I0566494

On the Back of a Motorbike

Stories and Poems from Southeast Asia

Edited by Kris Williamson

Printed in the United States of America

First Printing, 2016

ISBN 978-0-9967179-7-7
Library of Congress Control Number: 2016956049

Literary Concept
1731 Bonita Bluff CT
Ruskin, FL 33570
www.literaryconcept.com
editor@literaryconcept.com

Edited by Kris Williamson
Cover art by Moribayu

Ordering Information:
For details, contact the publisher at the e-mail address above.

Contents

Introduction
by Kris Williamson

Anyone who has been anywhere in Southeast Asia understands that there are nearly as many motorbikes as there are people. Or, at least, it certainly feels that way when on the road ... or sidewalk or anywhere else imaginable that you can fit a motorbike. They are everywhere!

As such, motorbikes are an inseparable part of everyday life, whether you live there and ride one daily or are just passing through the region and never even get on one. If you have ever used a pedestrian crosswalk in Vietnam, you will have paraded in front of a wall of revving bikes inching ever closer at the stoplight. If you have ever walked around Malaysian cities, you know that you need to watch for motorcyclists using the sidewalk as a way to skirt one-way streets or traffic jams. If you need a taxi in Indonesia but can't get one, you simply hop on the back of a stranger's motorbike—luggage and all—and be driven to your destination for a small fee. If you have ever attempted to cross the streets anywhere in Thailand, there's a good chance you were hit by one appearing out of nowhere.

But it isn't just the sheer number that makes them so prominent. Motorbikes are employed in so many ingenious ways. And for better or worse, Southeast Asian countries are the only places where you can find these uses. Family of four *and* the dog riding on a single motorbike? No problem. Motorbike drivers for hire at the push of an app to deliver pizza, post a package, take you somewhere, issue a court order, or bring a prostitute to your hotel room? Sure, why not?

Even criminals take advantage of the motorbike in ways that are not usually recreated elsewhere. Why risk getting outrun when snatching someone's bag when you can grab it off someone's shoulder while already on your getaway bike? Acid splash attackers? Machete-wielding maniacs? Suicide bombers? The motorbike has proven effective for these types as well.

Then there are the Saturday night city street races. The thrill of zigzagging around cars and trucks, fleeing from police, doing stunts with minimal safety precautions and risking lives for a little bit of fun. Oh, to be young and stupid.

This anthology has been in the works for many years, albeit at the idea-in-the-back-of-my-mind stage for the majority of that time. While I have many stories of my own about being on the back of a motorbike, I was curious about other people's experiences. But most people who I would have asked, I already knew their motorbike stories.

Coincidentally, the quarterly literary journal, *Anak Sastra*, with its Southeast Asian geographical theme, was approaching its 25th issue—a milestone worthy of doing something special. Instead of doing a themed issue, though, I decided to make it a proper anthology, where short stories, creative nonfiction and poetry—all features of the literary journal—could be presented in both print and digital formats with the restriction that it must have something to do with the phrase or the concept: "on the back of a motorbike." And obviously, all stories and poems needed to be set in or linked to one of the Southeast Asian countries. A call for submissions was sent out to all previous contributors to *Anak Sastra* and, to my relief, there were many good submissions. Too many, in fact.

In total there are 10 short fiction stories, 3 nonfiction accounts and 14 poems. The anthology is comprised of stories and poems from Indonesia, Malaysia, Singapore, Thailand, Laos, Cambodia, Vietnam and the Philippines. Sadly, Myanmar and Brunei are not represented in the book, though this is an unfortunate pattern in other likeminded anthologies and collections.

The stories and poems are as varied as the authors and their experiences. Poems range from fatalistic and autobiographical to funny and narrative. The nonfiction tales offer firsthand experience and insight into life in the region. And the short fiction includes everything from adventure and high jinks to self-discovery and love gone wrong. Whether written by locals, expats, travelers, or those among the global Diaspora, the stories and poems in this anthology crack open 27 different windows and doors into life around Southeast Asia and exude the rush of viewing the region as if from the back of a motorbike.

Have a read and enjoy the ride.

After Class
by Romalyn Ante

My uncle waited by the school fence

To pick me up one afternoon.

He wore that I'm-such-a-cool-uncle smile,

His teeth whiter than my uniform.

My heart thumped harder

Over the road bumps. Wrist-twist,

Wrist-twist, and the pleats of my skirt

Undulate in the airstream.

We took short-cuts – past the stone church,

Through the sidewalk stalls,

And over the bridge where locals

Chucked their dead pets goodbye.

He was the kind of uncle who stole fruits

From his own shop, behind his strict,

Chinese wife.

My pocket filled with rambutans.

He'd mimic the landlady, his arms akimbo,

and laugh at the cheapskate, bald *sapatero*.

He'd give you his helmet, joked that his head

Had already hardened from many beatings.

After so many years, he'd be there, gulping

All the *Welcome Home* alcohol, and insisting

He'd tour you around, take you here and there,

On his rusty motorbike. Just like before.

Road Trip
by Romalyn Ante

Night breeze on my face.

Orchids-scented.

We speed along the Mekong,

your blue-black hair

brushes at my cheek.

It's the season of flying lanterns

and candle-lit baskets on the river.

The nocturnal world swirls

with pretty women in silk,

spiced delicacies on the grill.

My grasp tightens

around your tensed abdomen

And the horizon hazes like fireflies,

metropolitan noise becomes

our background music.

I lay my chin on your shoulder,

embrace the heat

of your leather jacket,

until there's only you, me,

and the night.

This Is My Husband
by Lindsay Boyd

Not quite three years into their wedlock—their daughter had turned two a few months before while their son was yet a babe—Lac and Thuy were lying in the conjugal bed at the family home outside the old trading hub of Hoi An when Lac turned to his wife with the notion to confess something that had been uppermost in his mind for a considerable time but that he hadn't had the heart to confide until then.

Prone on his back, his left forearm resting upon his forehead, he glanced at Thuy, lightly touching the auburn-tinged black hair splayed upon her bare shoulders. He thought she might be asleep, in which case his revelation would go unheard. He decided to venture forth anyway, in case she was sentient in some shape or form.

"I don't feel the desire for you I once did."

His tone was measured. He might have just made the most commonplace of observations. Having spoken, Lac listened out. Only the whirring of a below ceiling level fan and the regular breathing of the two children, asleep beneath a mosquito net on the other side of the room, interfered with the quiet.

He doubted Thuy had heard him until she turned on her back thirty seconds after he spoke. There a slowness to the movement that induced him to wonder if she had she seen this coming. Had she now identified the reason why he had, for months, appeared dismissive of the efforts she put in to be an ideal spouse? She propped on her left elbow and gave him an eloquent look. Would he please explain exactly what he meant? He met her gaze, but she waited in vain for him to elaborate.

To abet her ongoing study of the elusive English language, Thuy occasionally picked up an English language book, magazine or newspaper. An article recently browsed in a lifestyle magazine examined the issue of sex in the lives of couples after the birth of children. Inevitably, love lives underwent critical changes with this eventuality, the American author of the piece theorized.

Thuy, however, failed to see it as a matter of importance, either for her and Lac or any of the couples she knew who were now, like them, rearing children. Of course everything altered on the appearance of children, not simply on the sex side of the equation. But she never gave it much thought. Nor did she and Lac ever waste time discussing it.

Now that he had admitted something extraordinary—extraordinary if she had heard him right—she wondered if they should have talked it over, as the pundits discussed it in the written piece. It was clear, after all, what desire Lac was referring to: the desire of his flesh for her flesh. Before she could put her thoughts into words or offer assurances of any kind, he spoke again.

"I've become attracted to men."

Lac believed his earliest memories were, in essence, no different to those the vast majority in the nation could lay claim to. Like everyone, he became familiar with the whiskered, kindly features of the so-called father of the nation, rice paddies slaved upon by conical-hatted figures from dawn to dusk—tracts of them sat a short distance from the heart of town—and motorbikes.

Memory, for Lac, decisively kicked in around the age of eight. The few remembrances he could call up before then related to his father's motorbike. He saw the younger him ensconced upon it, safely cocooned by one or both parents as they careered around the old and modern parts of the town and the outskirts. Sometimes the contented trio rode the additional few kilometers to the beach at Cua Dai, there partaking of oversweet refreshments before journeying homeward.

Did every child born and doted upon in the land conjure similar tales in later years? Did they speak also of graduating from the safe front position of the motorbike—balanced in those reliable parental arms—to the more independent rear, clinging to the back of mom or dad? Probably. Until finally, *cum laude*, they assumed the helm. It was a collective consciousness of memory borne upon two skinny wheels.

A more overtly personal element of Lac's upbringing concerned his parents. His father was appreciably older than his mother—no less than twenty-seven years older.

"Your dad's old enough to be your granddad," was a quip heard now and again when the old man brought him to or from school.

Lac rarely responded when someone said that to him. He loved his chain-smoking, rice-wine-drinking father as much as he did his svelte mother, if not more. Nor would anything ever compare with the experience of riding through town with the old boy, hands wrapped about the other's big belly. Alas, Gau drank and smoked more than was good for him and discarded this mortal coil at the age of sixty-four. His only child was eleven.

The widowed mother, then thirty-seven, redoubled her efforts, not wishing to see her son worse off for the absence of the parent who formed an indispensable side of their complete triangle. The deceased possessed a yen for alcohol and tobacco—like untold numbers of men—but he was a good man at heart, no wife terrorizer when he'd had a few, and an affectionate father to their pride and joy.

Toh, figuratively speaking, brought Lac back to her hip. For the youngster it seemed as if the days when she literally walked around, indoors and outdoors, with him either on her favored left hip or less often her right, recurred.

She *must* have carried him in that way, being one of those mothers who eschewed separation from their little ones for lengthy periods of the day. They trusted in the warmth their bodies generated, considering it the best love and security, tickets to happy, fulfilling lives. The fathers pampered and held too, in equally fond ways, replaying for their sons and daughters scenes derived from their own experience, now imprinted on their DNA.

Whenever, growing up, Lac beheld a mother with her child at her hip, or a father with his own in his big arms, he understood better the sheer power, the inviolability, of the bond of family in the land of his birth. For the parents, the children were everything.

Odd then that something didn't feel right. The sense increased after Gau's death, as if the event let loose harbingers kept in check up to then but that bubbled away unacknowledged beneath the surface. No one could say for how long. Something in this life was too regimented for Lac's liking. He reckoned his father smarted under the strictures too, but the extent of the elder's rebellion was limited.

Gau's outlet was the standard male playthings combined with a whimsical sense of humor. The son also smoked and drank but never to excess. The characteristic he inherited from his progenitor in full measure was the latter's whimsy. Lac entertained friends at school with *sotto voce* summations of this or that teacher on the staff.

Amazed at his daring, his peers would muffle their amusement in the palms of their hands. He especially targeted those he deemed likely to be highly placed in the hierarchy, members of the People's Committees and so on. His estimates as to status were generally spot on.

At 7:20 on the dot every school morning, music with chipmunk voices at the forefront blared from loudspeakers at a neighborhood preschool. If he happened not to be up and about himself by the hour, Lac abruptly shifted position in bed and blocked his ears with his pillow to shut out the rousing anthem. His liking for impromptu mimicry of the chipmunk choruses was another source of amusement to his fellows.

Go to the beach. Four simple words but special to Lac because they were the first in the curious language he committed to memory. To the south of Cua Dai on a quiet stretch of beach front road between there and the developing An Bang, there were many signs bearing the imperative. Strategically positioned at the start of narrow trails that led up and over sandy ridges and down to the clear waters of the South China Sea, the words on them were directional as much as imperative.

Gau taught them to his son, but his English pronunciation was as wayward as Lac's would later become. In his mouth *go to the beach* sounded like *goat bitch*. *Goat bitch* became akin to a password between the man and boy, something to be sniggered at whether a beach visit was on the cards or not.

Outings to the beach, or anywhere of note for that matter, became fewer in number when the former threesome was reduced to a twosome. Toh had her hands in many pots—she engaged in activities as diverse as baking, a *bánh mi* stall, a vegetable stall and a launderette run out of the home—and needed to keep them there as well as expand her interests when she and Lac had to do without Gau's financial input, erratic as it was.

Lac happily went off by himself when Toh deemed him of age. Declaring his work done for the day, he rode to Cua Dai with friends or alone. From there he proceeded south or north, often taking the northerly direction and winding up in Da Nang. Loudspeakers clamored at the city's beach showpiece Pham Van Dong much as they did at the preschool near home. But no chipmunks were to be heard in this Muzak. What he was compelled to listen to by the broad foreshore were in large part instrumental versions of old Western popular tunes.

Amid the late afternoon crowds at the Eastern Sea Park, the hordes of bare-chested men and women demure in colorful, conservatively cut swimwear, he stood out by dint of his unkempt hair (he preferred the mop-top style to the ultra short at the back and sides look many of his contemporaries favored). The fact that he was unwashed after his labor added to the unprepossessing sight.

He never imagined there would come a day when he would dress in all-white—or all-black, if the heat didn't render the preference out of the question—and frolic on the My Khe sands with his white or cream-clad bride in his arms, beaming at the camera for their future descendants. This was a common sight along the My Khe expanse.

A few minutes spent watching a showy couple enact their version of "Ring around the Rosie" and climbing upon each other at the water's edge was more than enough for him. He beat a retreat fast, usually stopping around the Cua Dai side of An Bang and following one of the 'Goat Bitch' trails to the sand. In the refreshingly unpeopled environs he eyed the circular *thúngs* that sufficed for fishing boats and lost himself in the yellow-blue light and the gentle sound of lapping waves.

In spite of his conviction he had his moment. He donned all-white and held a woman for the wielder of a camera and his light reflector associate. The woman's name was Thuy. What most appealed to him about her before he broke the ice and made an approach was her impressive form on the motorbike she used to scoot around Hui Ba Trung, Thung Kiet, Nguyen Chi Tranh and other central parts of Hoi An.

Thuy laughed at the compliment. They were visiting over fruit shakes at a Western-style bakery on Hai Ba Trung.

"What do you do?"

"I'm a trained electrician," he answered, deftly wiping away a speck of drink glued to the right corner of his mouth. "But I haven't worked as one for ... How long? Two years? Three years?"

Thuy studied the handsome face till he understood she was waiting for him to answer her question.

"I work in a restaurant. I help with the cooking and serving."

"Where?"

He gestured toward the west, fixing the location in or near the old town.

"A restaurant for tourists or locals?"

"Both. We get both."

"Then you must know some English?"

Lac gave her a bashful look. "No. A couple of words only. Goat bitch." Thuy smiled at his explanation of the witticism. She had passed the same signs herself on journeys along that stretch of road. "My boss is the one who speaks English. He is an English-speaking man."

His inability was more incongruous to Thuy when she heard that. But it was just one of the enigmatic man's foibles. She learned about others little by little. Far from putting her off, or undermining her growing affection for him, in a decisive way they enhanced his appeal.

The restaurant connection fascinated her. One of her dreams for the future revolved around the establishment of a restaurant downtown. Lac knew little about the business side of the enterprise, but Thuy gathered much in conversation with his boss, to whom Lac introduced her. The proprietor picked up on her evident resolve and gladly enlightened her.

She was a determined young woman, as resolute as Lac was free and easy in his approach to life. The second of three daughters, she demonstrated an aptitude for business in her late teens and from then on applied herself to the acquisition of skills that stood her in good stead in a burgeoning tourism industry.

She possessed less of a natural affinity for the requisite language component of her studies. How could she make a career in the tourist trade without good knowledge of English? But she soldiered on gamely and grew more confident in her language ability. From that eureka point on, she reflected on the time when she went out of her way to conceal herself from native English speakers rather than draw attention to her ineptitude, a period when her confidence couldn't have been lower, with not a little amusement.

Lac would've preferred the prenuptial photo shoot to have gone ahead with none but himself, Thuy and the two-man crew on hand and for it to have proceeded at a less conspicuous time—for example early in the morning, rather than the late afternoon 'rush' hour. He gained his wish on neither hand.

There was no chance of inconspicuousness at 5pm on a brutally hot Friday in June. The beach at the end of Pham Van Dong was overrun. Passersby, complete strangers every single one, gawked at the 'stars' of the show as if they were a prince and princess, distant descendants of the country's defunct royal court. Even when he removed his jacket, Lac sweated bullets in his white shirt, pants and shoes.

Off-putting as he found the scrutiny of the beachgoers, he was more painfully aware of the relatives and friends observing from a way off. Had they been elsewhere he may not have had the titanic struggle with Thuy's weight that he did when it came time for the obligatory 'crossing the threshold' or 'at the threshold' shot in the series. The light reflector boy intervened in time, sparing everyone the ignominy of the bride going face down on the damp, soft-packed sand.

Had she gained weight during the two years of their courtship? Lac light-heartedly broached the question in conversation with others later. But the near miss was not such a laughing matter for some, foremost among them Thuy's one-legged father, Thien. He never warmed to the slovenly, unfocussed lump his daughter chose to wed and firmly believed she would ultimately rue her choice.

"What about what *you* want to do? Does he show any interest in that?"

Remarks such as this did not go down well with his daughter. Nor were they entirely fair on Lac. Fortunately, then, his efforts to dissuade her were confined to scattered comments of the kind.

She may well have added pounds, Lac thought, sizing her up *au naturel*. But in the first couple of years of their marriage, the figure she cut on two wheels went on impressing, whether she rode around in short summer pants, a cotton knee-length frock in which she looked touchingly girlish or camouflaged from head to toe in polka dot fabrics. She chose the complete covering on the hottest days in order to counter the sun's effect on her fair skin.

Lac left the restaurant and resumed his trade, which kept him busy around town. He was in no hurry to have children. He even suggested to Thuy that they wait to begin a family until she was more established in her undertakings. This rankled would-be grandfather Thien, who limped about the house and declared it a further instance of his son-in-law's unreliability. The recently wedded pair took up with her family in the sprawling house a few kilometers out of town on the inland road to Da Nang. No domestic issue escaped open discussion for long living in such close proximity.

Thuy wanted to bear children sooner rather than later and, at the same time, preserve her business interests. From what she knew about Western ways, women in those countries coped ably with this motherhood/career balance. She pushed herself to accomplish the same.

She was close to the age of twenty seven when their daughter was born. Her dream of a restaurant in the heart of Hoi An had become reality and, not long after the birth of the girl, she opened a travel agency around the corner from the eating house. In another shrewd business move, she won her mum and dad over to the idea of adding rooms to the side and rear of the family home, converting it into a homestay.

These endeavors demanded imagination and staying power. Thuy was up for the challenge. A baby to care for on top of that was no trifle, but she wasn't lacking for help, even if the one she would have expected to carry a considerable part of the burden was often nowhere to be seen.

"I'm busy with my electrical work," Lac said, positing this as the main reason for his prolonged absences. He also visited his widowed mother, who lived near the beach at Cua Dai, frequently. If these commitments meant missing out on time with his 'acquired' family, how could he help that?

His wife's family liked to come together for the middle of the day meal in the courtyard at the front of the house. Generally they got started between 11:30am and noon. Sometimes Lac showed when the others were chomping away. Other times everyone else would've eaten and dispersed, leaving the partly empty dishes of white rice, meat, fish, vegetables and condiments arrayed about the long tables and at the mercy of flies. Either way no one paid him heed when he rode into the courtyard and removed his helmet to better appraise the scene.

Once fatherhood—he took philosophically his earlier than hoped for assumption of the role—fell to his lot, his tardiness increased, not only at meal times but also in his attendance at the range of family rituals. "It's like I don't have a husband," Thuy was heard to lament.

Thien sympathized with his middle daughter but for her sake rarely articulated his disdain. One day, however, when an electrical job in one of the rooms on the homestay side required Lac's know-how and he lingered on afterward for the commencement of the middle of the day repast, the one-legged man took him to task before the entire family.

"Are *you* a member of this family?"

Lac's preferred recourse when dealing with his father-in-law's harangues was unflappable silence. Being quick witted, he was also not averse to making rejoinders that could incite the older man to greater wrath. This time his initial inclination was to opt for the silent treatment.

"Do *you* have a wife and daughter?"

In Lac's estimation this was one too many stupid questions. "If they haven't vanished off the face of the earth since the last time I looked, yes."

"Then when are you going to start behaving like you do?"

Lac eyed Thuy, eating with her mouth close to her bowl and eyes averted, and their tomboyish daughter in quick succession. He had a riposte ready but bit back on it on remembering an occasion in the recent past when a sardonic remark of his went down badly. "Vietnamese husbands and wives don't have sex for pleasure," he had said then, grinning into his noodles. "They have sex to keep the party happy."

Thien's tea-colored complexion approximated a shade of red. He had been as schooled as any young man of his generation. The loss of his limb occurred when he was a boy during the American War and the family was caught in a stray firefight between the combatants. To have to listen to this imbecile, this Hoi An hick, make fun of everything in this way ... it was really too much.

Notwithstanding his crimped physical desire, Lac credited Thuy's get up and go career wise. He doubted he could have mustered the same even had he not been a natural-born lazy bones and bothered to master rudimentary English when the golden opportunity stared him in the face.

While he worked desultorily at his trade, sometimes easing his way into the marital chamber at the close of a day with nicks or somewhat graver cuts on his hands and forearms, the result of ham-fistedness or out-and-out poor workmanship, she excelled at everything she did. From the ever increasing distance between them, Lac pondered where she came up with her ideas.

She was several months pregnant with their son when she tracked down and submitted a potential host profile to a web based organization that teamed foreign travelers with hosts willing to provide them room and board in exchange for a few hours work a day. In a sense it was a logical extension of the homestay concept, which was reaping dividends for the family. But Lac never saw it coming and offered his wife kudos, unaware as he did of the categorical change this move on Thuy's part would bring about in the lives of everyone in the close-knit family.

The foreigners began coming thick and fast, at the rate of roughly one a month. Statuesque Bridget from Belgium was the first. Thuy arranged for her to teach English to the preschoolers in the kindergarten next door to the house. Peppi, from Canada, assisted with the running of the homestay and closed her fifteen-day visit with the painting of a mural on the wall on the kindergarten side. Alfredo, a Spaniard, was helpful in multiple areas. There wasn't a task he baulked at, including caring for the children, a willingness Trang relied upon when other options were scarce.

Every volunteer who came evinced the same spirit and the family and extended family, not excluding Lac, met each one with uniform good grace and friendliness. But Lac's decided interest lay in the males among the visitors, a fact not lost on Thuy and the others. He was attentive to the females too, but it was the young men who garnered extra effort and time.

It was hard work establishing a bond without a shared tongue, but he did his best. Xin, a local boy who worked at the homestay, sometimes translated what Lac wished to say to the helpers. Conversation could also be facilitated through the aid of a translation application on someone's phone or laptop computer. A far from ideal contingency but it was better than nothing.

In the early period the volunteer Lac was most drawn to was the South American Garcia. He sought a parting, going away portrait or three of each one of the guys (the girls he never bothered with in that respect), preferably with him in the frame too, his arm around the waist or shoulders of the lad. As early as a week or so out from the Colombian's eventual departure, he pressed upon Garcia for a portrait at every turn. Come the actual day Lac had several on his phone with which to remember him by.

Handsome, in a disheveled, rustic kind of way not unlike Lac, perennially tan Pete, a central California native, traveled direct to the homestay from Da Nang Airport. Thuy greeted him affably and, after showing him to a downstairs room in the house, fixed him a mid-evening snack.

"Anything I can help you with here, y'all let me know," he said, before calling it a night. "Your name again?"

"Thuy."

The messages he had received while setting up the placement had been signed "Thuy, Lac and family" or "Thuy and Lac." He incorrectly assumed the Thuy he corresponded with was the man of the household.

"Oh. *You're* Thuy?"

"Yes," she said, smiling at his surprise.

"Where's your husband?"

"He's not here now. Tomorrow you will meet."

Pete reiterated his readiness to help wherever there was a need to Thuy while scoffing a pancake for breakfast the next morning.

"I make lousy pancakes," Thuy said, apologizing for the finished product. "My husband is the cook."

Pete waved aside her misgiving. "Tastes okay to me, babe."

The buzzing of an electrical tool announced an immediate need when he reappeared after a post-meal wash and shave. An extension was being added to the reception and restaurant area, an uncomplicated addition Lac contributed to.

"What can I do?" Pete asked Thuy as he sat before her computer monitor.

She looked at the trio of men laboring on the extension. "You can help my husband."

By simple elimination Pete deduced that he must be the one with the shock of dark hair. The other two he had glimpsed the night before but not had the opportunity to speak with. He approached Lac and introduced himself, receiving a firm grasp of his offered hand in response.

Pete was older by several years than the majority of the volunteers who preceded him at the homestay. In part because of that he exerted a different, somehow stronger, attraction on thirty-something Lac than any of the past helpers, with the possible exception of Garcia. Undeniably, Lac also recognized in the knockabout American a kindred spirit. Within twenty-four hours he was tapping on the visitor's door at odd hours, fashioning an intimacy more appropriate for friends well acquainted.

Working outdoors Lac often pulled his shirts up to the breastbone to stave off the heat. He did the same one day for Pete, but with the object of revealing his latest skin afflictions. He sought physical nearness whenever he could and transmitted playful touches as the other worked or ate his meals. Presumption that rattled some of the young male volunteer brigade did not faze Pete, who had seen it all and more during the years he led a vagabond lifestyle in his homeland.

But there were more twists in store for him pertaining to the union of this Vietnamese couple. "Thuy's your wife, dude," he said to Lac, after it became clear he resided elsewhere. "How come you don't live with her?"

When he understood what he was being asked, Lac smiled. How to explain he had not lived at the house for most of the last year. The fallout from his confession to Thuy had been swift. It enabled Thien to begin a process of 'banishment' of the son-in-law.

Bao, a young family friend, was roped in to work around the premises and assume the role of ostensible father of the children. He, like the one he substituted, had a propensity to wear his shirts and singlets like crop tops on sweltering days, but there the resemblance ended. Within months, largely in secret, he began sharing the much happier Thuy's bed.

"Where is your husband?" Pete, not yet wise to the whole story, asked her at one of the first evening meals he shared with the family.

"Gone home. *This* is my husband!" She indicated Bao, sitting beside her, apparently oblivious to what was being said about him.

Effectively, Thuy and Lac remained married in name only, a state of affairs satisfactory to both.

"When you have free time come to my place," Xin translated for Pete on Lac's behalf. It was lunchtime, two and a half weeks into the American's stay. Lac had been touchy-feely with the visitor to an extreme degree as he tried to concentrate on his food.

"You're a married man," Pete replied, in jest. "What would your wife think? Anyway I don't know where you live or how I'd get there."

Lac, standing next to his motorbike preparatory to heading back out to work, indicted the rear part of the seat.

Wombs
by D.R.L. Heywood-Lonsdale

Your best friend came from a father's

womb, a 1967 Volkswagen beetle convertible

that flitted between his girlfriend's house—with

the mosaic pool and wind chimes—and viola

lessons, staccato strong and quick the way he

would die one summer like the snapping of a string

she felt in her bellybutton. Years later in Germany or

India or Laos she'll peel herself from other people's

parents and crawl into the backseat with her lover, her

dog or alone of this car shipped thousands of

miles, better than the back of a motorbike or the bars

of a *tuk-tuk* or a chicken bus without a handkerchief. Better

than your student's womb, the oval of desks where his

classmates questioned God and man's addiction to

spinning stories Rumpelstiltskin how

the lion and lamb could be forged by one guy how

the gays, the blacks, the Muslims each a rat-a-tat-tat

into your student's skin until the rounds were empty

like his eyes. The ten-year-old atheist birthed from a

philosophy lesson confused to sad to silent at

home too respectful to let his parents know

they were wrong. This—gift—of education builds walls

when you tell him it's a battering ram. While your own

womb, the green juice and mint mojito coffees in southern

California sweat out your linen blazer too European for

Kogi tacos and feel in the pads of your fingers a

rush of getting lost in a canyon after dark

again. Arrogance that birthed a quiet and self-deprecating

grown-up only to find that you're the only one changed;

to realize you hoped he would ask about your book or

the man you learned to trust or how you broke your first

bone when he is more interested in weed and drawing

on his walls with chalk; you are surprised to find

that you still get jealous just a niggling, the shadow

of an ache, a poppy seed in your teeth

which makes you shy to smile. You wanted to cry

for your student as you watched him embittered

let down by his classmates who mocked his defense

of free will; the god of spaghetti frees all, they said, and

writes in our alphabet too. Or when you heard the news

to tell your best friend that at least he could never let her

down and no need to return to old places with people

and old postcards and hope that we have changed or

stood still at the same rate like polar caps or else

disastrous consequences. That she is, in fact, luckier

than the rest of us who can never crawl back into our

mothers' buttery wombs in Nam Ha, especially one

that can open its uterine wall to the skies

to show her the stars as he grows.

The Truth about Mo
by Paul GnanaSelvam

All truth passes through three stages, a subtle thought vibrates in Rukku's head. It is a line she had read on *Facebook* and memorized. Sighing at the sight of black moss mapped across her kitchen walls, Rukku wipes the counter with a dry rag. She ladles a spoonful of coffee into her mug and stirs it slowly. All around the village, motorbikes have sprung to life and fill the streets noisily like an army on a march. She looks out from the window of her rented home, the extended back portion of a large house, and notices that Ramesh has not returned from the temple. The modest porch is strewn with dry mango leaves brought in by the hot air that swept down from greater Kuala Lumpur. *All truth passes through three stages*, she repeats, the bitter, hot coffee searing her taste buds.

First, it is ridiculed.

Dragging a chair toward the kitchen window, she leans her elbows on the counter and cups her narrow chin. The allamandas that Ramesh planted are in full bloom. She often teases him for his liking of flowers as being effeminate. But how she wishes she hadn't said such things now. She should have listened to him, especially on the day Mo turned sixteen and declared that he wanted a motorbike and nothing less.

Ramesh did not buy the idea. He was reluctant. He said only he knew what boys did on the back of their motorbikes. The days that followed were the most unfriendly ones, with both father and son sulking around each other. Blinded by affection, I took Mo's side. I should not have scoffed at Ramesh, putting akin his fear for the fast and dangerous to the

32

liking of his effeminate hobby, horticulture. I downplayed his opinions, disregarding his experiences as an office boy who moved around town on a motorbike himself. I failed to realize that his fatherly concerns for the safety of his son came from his awareness of the devilry that was stirring Mo's hormones.

"The first two weeks, that's all," Ramesh pointed out. "The first two weeks they'd be fine. After that, once they get used to the machine, they will surrender themselves to it. They will hardly notice the time as it passed by. Their adrenaline will be shooting through the roof. They think they are invulnerable. It's total ecstasy, I say," I thought I heard Ramesh choking as he spoke. "And he would not be left alone. They'd come, in gangs and in pairs. They'd whisper secret initiations into his ears. They would block his ears and cloud his mind. I've seen it happen. Too many times, Rukku. Will you please listen to me?" he pleaded.

"But Pa, our son has come of age," I chirped inconsiderately. "He should be doing what all sixteen year olds do. He needs to move into the world. Absorb the universe. Become a man. Unless he is given the motorbike, he will not earn his freedom. He will not be at liberty to make decisions. He will not be able to solve problems. Or take ownership of his life and learn responsibility," I debated while Ramesh sat on the sofa and lit a cigarette.

"On the road, there are dangers he must learn to look out for. We cannot keep protecting him, Ramesh. Our boy must grow up. On top of that, he could send me to work. I'm tired of waiting for the feeder buses. Mo could drop me off at the LRT station on his way to school. Stop laughing. Ramesh! I could go to the market on the weekends while you're off on your part-time work. I do not want to depend on you all the time.

There are millions of boys out there and even girls of Mo's age who already have a motorbike. I think you are being paranoid, simply paranoid, Ramesh. Let go, Pa. He will be fine. And we can afford to buy a motorbike, can't we?"

There was no reply from Ramesh. He got up to leave. I got agitated. "I just don't want you to turn Mo into one of your flowers," I shouted angrily at him.

"Are you mocking me?" Ramesh asked, pushing the cigarette butt into the ashtray. "I am talking about my only son," he retorted. "I'm concerned for his safety. I want him to remain as Mo. To hold my hand when my legs give way and my vision frays. He has to light my pyre when my time is up. He is my only hope. And who will see to your needs when I am gone? There are hundreds, thousands, no doubt millions riding around town on motorbikes, but we've got only one son," Ramesh growled in a stupor. "Don't you dare mock me!" he warned.

All truth passes through three stages. First, it is ridiculed. Rukku closes her eyes. It has been two weeks since Ramesh had spoken to her.

Then, it is violently opposed.

She closes her eyes again and strains her neck against the chair's headrest. She feels a minute's relief from her stiff shoulders and neck. She sips more coffee. She catches sight of the allamanda again and smiles ruefully. Their bright yellow hues that used to warm her heart now remain bland and neglected. She notices that they've grown so wild that they've climbed to the top of the mango tree. This huge shrub overtaking the garden grew from tiny saplings that Mo brought home from school one day. It was a class project designed to inculcate in children a sense of dutiful love to all living things. When the saplings outgrew their soil bags, Ramesh replanted them along the hedges that separated the big house from their compound. Small birds nested on the bushels—house sparrows and humming birds. There were a dozen or so new nests hidden in the bushes, Rukku remembers. Soon the compound will be filled with the fluttering noise of the birds tending to their new hatchlings.

Ramesh was right all along ...

The motorbike arrived one Friday evening. Mo was delighted. He ran in circles and hugged us silly. Such is the sweetness of a child's gratitude. We took it in, mindful that danger awaited Mo in dark hidden corners. Ramesh began to teach Mo a thing or two about road safety, motorbike etiquette and maintenance. In the evenings he took Mo to show him the simple routes he should be taking—from home to school, from home to my workplace and from home to the market. Ramesh applied holy ash on the polished chrome fenders every morning. It tickles me though, when I think of it, for it annoyed Mo. But Mo had other things on his mind.

In no time, he threw away his books and set his heart on the machine. First, a large sticker of a hissing cobra appeared on the front flaps of his motorbike. Then he started pestering for more money to spend on his modifications. Ramesh refused. Mo turned down what I offered, saying it was insignificant. "It's a new motorbike," I kept repeating. But it fell on deaf ears. Mo grew remorseful. He snapped angrily at his father. All he could talk to me about was modifications to add swiftness to his motorbike. *Ma*, he called out from the front of his motorbike one Sunday, *if only I could add field coils to the chain and calipers*, though I could not envision his words, *we would reach the market in no time.* "But there is no hurry. You have ample time," I told him. "The market is not going anywhere," I joked.

Three months later, I began to grow worried when I didn't hear his motorbike revving on the porch by midnight. Police summons arrived in the mail. Ramesh had to settle them. The late nights out with his new friends estranged Mo from us. He hardly touches his dinners anymore. He is curled too tightly in his blankets to be shaken awake for the Sunday markets. On weekdays he leaves for school at half-past-seven in school uniform and arrives home in the late evening in casual attire—none that I remember paying for. And he has stopped asking us for money. I didn't share my observations with Ramesh until the day that Mo had to be adjudicated.

Neighbors informed Ramesh that they had seen Mo riding his motorcycle during school hours in the quiet residential areas. Sometimes they'd seen him parked along the roads or junctions, waiting for others to show up on their motorbikes. They left after discreet exchanges of small packets and notes during pretentious conversations. A visit to the school confirmed that Mo had been playing truant. Ramesh flew into a rage when Mo admitted that he planned to drop out. He stood defiantly against Ramesh, chest to chest, father to son. Ramesh unbuckled his belt and started striking Mo with all his might. Mo stood like a stubborn ass, staring. I tried to intervene but knew the better to stay out of this.

The beating subsided and Mo left the living room without a word. I followed him. Much to my dismay, Mo took out a pack of cigarettes and lit one. He stood by the window in his room taking out rolls of money from his pockets. I gulped a few times and approached him quietly. A new sense of fear clouded my mind at the realization of Mo's changes. Sensing my dread, Mo laughed, threw the rolls of money on his bed and said, "Ma, this is everything. Life is useless without money." He took off his T-shirt and opened the windows. He shrugged and pushed away my hands when I wanted to touch him. Amid the rising pink and purple welts, I noticed how much my skinny boy had put on weight. The welts stood atop his muscles like stamp marks. It was then I realized that the motorbike had taken away my boy and given me a brazen young man. Ramesh was wrong to have struck him. But I also knew I was losing Mo.

Mo left school the following year—before he turned seventeen—much to Ramesh's disappointment. Ramesh became more of a recluse from then on. He would turn down Mo's gifts and would take no part in Mo's revelries or invitations to eat out together. He would lower his head when walking and rarely spoke to anyone. His voice had become heavy with a worried undertone. He abandoned his garden. His allamandas grew beyond reach.

All truth passes through three stages. First, it is ridiculed. Then it is violently opposed. Lastly, you surrender to it. Truth is accepted as self-evident.

The last fifteen days have been terrible. Grief arrives, unannounced on swift winds, like a huge storm that unfurls its contents—hail, thunder and rain—at once. It uproots and damages everything in its path. It is blind to everything. It has no mercy on whoever it crosses paths with. It pelts the soul mercilessly and leaves everlasting pain. Rukku pulls out some tissues and sneezes into them. She closes her eyes again and shakes her head. She looks at the clock and rolls her eyes at it. "What's the hurry?" She mumbles. She lifts a finger and makes a counterclockwise twirling movement and giggles. She adds some sugar to her lukewarm coffee. After taking a sip, she cups her mouth and brings a hand up to her chest, stroking it. The tears break free like opened floodgates and blur her vision.

It was Deepavali. Mo stayed at home for the longest period of time since the motorbike had arrived two years earlier. "Let's celebrate," he announced. I filled a whole tin full of *achi murukku* and *atharasam*, which puffed up on the surface of the hot oil like lucky stars from the deep wok. A canopy was erected on our little compound, its peripheries bordered by chasing lights. With Ramesh's consent, Mo had invited his new friends over. These were a total contradiction to the neat, timid boys in pressed uniforms and plain hairstyles I was accustomed to. These were stylish men who arrived in polished cars, heavily tinted windshields, wore excessive jewelry, dressed fashionably and sported identical tattoos of a hissing cobra. Ramesh pulled me aside and lamented that Mo had certainly learned a thing or two about feasting. Fireworks lit up the village sky, cartons of beer cans floated in a plastic tub filled with ice and lots of curried and barbequed meat were served. His friends joked about Mo's interest in a girl I had never met. I smiled politely, knowing that Mo was only nineteen and still loved the dangerous life he had chosen.

I was perturbed when one of the boys suddenly ran out to his car and produced a roll of fire crackers that the Chinese used to ward off evil spirits on the eve of the winter solstice. A few others joined him. They tied one end of the coil to a branch of the mango tree and lined it in a zigzag manner across the road outside the gate. When it went off, it was loud enough to shove all evil into Hell. From within the thick, sulfuric fog appeared a buff, middle-aged Chinese man, bedecked in a thick, gold chain carrying a large hamper. He was followed by his wife and two young children. Unlike the others, he was modestly dressed in khaki shorts, a pair of sandals and a white sweat shirt. A long serpentine beast was tattooed on his right arm. Mo received him as if a great sage had arrived at our home, while the other boys stood by reverently. When he left, I found a thick wad of 100 ringgit notes in the hamper.

Mo was his normal self throughout the party. He was not even drunk. He helped me clean up the compound and ate his dinner last. I served his food. He left home to visit his friends thereafter. In a funny way he asked if I would be awake when he returned home that night. But I was too tired. I woke up when I heard Mo calling for me. It was 4am. I had overslept. I quickly got up and checked his room. It was empty. So was the porch. We waited for three nights for Mo. There was no sign of him. His friends were silent. Ramesh was silent. The neighbors grew silent. Three nights later, a policeman knocked on our door and asked if we were Mo's parents. The stocky policeman looked uncomfortable and distressed, having had to convey the unpleasant news. For the first few minutes we were distracted, probably saved from a cardiac arrest by trying to discern his words. "PasenssPiss, PasenssPiss," he blurted. Ramesh had to repeat the words after him, Patience Please". The revolving blue lights from the strobe of the patrol car were bright enough to stir the neighbors awake and fill our porch. Maybe they too knew that Mo's revving of the motorbike was never to be heard again.

At the mortuary the mouth-full-of-tongue officer kept asking us to remain calm as we were ushered to the cold chambers to identify Mo's body. From a file of papers he flashed a picture of a tattooed cobra. It annoyed me, as he kept pushing the picture onto our faces, even to the hospital staff at the mortuary. "Don't you have anything else to show?" I shouted at him angrily. It stunned him for a moment. He quickly put the picture into the file that he was carrying while searching for words. "A finger, a toe, or a mole and scar, a face," my voice broke. "Why don't you show everyone a face? Show me a face, damn you!" I screeched and kicked the medicine dispenser down the corridor. "PasenssPiss, PasenssPiss, madam," he pleaded. I calmed down. "He is my son," I told him.

Ramesh stared me down as he signed the release forms at the mortuary.

With the help of Mo's friends, we brought his body home, wrapped in hospital sheets. Ramesh was too distraught to oversee the funeral arrangements. Thus, I took over the responsibility. I hardened my soul. By the time our relatives had arrived to console me, my tears were gone. Though everyone protested, I braved up and offered to bathe him myself. In the midst of grief, I found lesions, swelling and clumsily stitched punctures on his body. The men who bathed him whispered about bullets and assassinations. I closed my ears. I rubbed soap on his cold body and sprinkled warm water over him, feeling every inch of my only son. His skin was rough with hair, and his muscles were hard. When they turned him, the birth mark on his buttocks remained a dark splotch of green. Everyone who visited me when Mo was born claimed it was a good sign. "You are lucky," they had told me. I laid his head on my lap and gazed at his face one last time. I could hardly recognize him anymore. All I could do was dress his bare body in sandalwood paste and perfumed rose water, like marinated chicken prepped for the frying pan.

People talked. People talked a lot about Mo. Was he the perfect bait, a victim of his allegiance to the triad boss who he served chicken and mutton curry during Deepavali? The rumors were thick, and it wafted around the funeral tent. What took them three days to return him to his family? Did he really die in an accident? Wasn't he the one who would rev his motorbike in the middle of the night and disrupt everyone's peace and quiet? He did not listen to his parents. Wasn't he a drug pusher, greedy and selfish? Imagine how many parents lost their children to his business? How many wives would have lost their husbands? Children their fathers? He chose his path and karma returned its wages. All he gave his parents was nothing but grief. Blame the mother. She spoiled him. She gifted him the motorbike, and it took him to his untimely grave!

Rukku knew something was amiss. The rumors were not true. There were roadblocks all over town that night. Maybe Mo was not carrying an illegal substance. Maybe he was arrested on suspicion. Was he tipped off by those he trusted? There was no proof he was carrying drugs. And the reports mentioned sudden death caused by an accident. It bewildered Ramesh, their relatives and Mo's friends. Mo's possessions had all gone missing. Nothing was returned except for Mo's motorbike a week later. His gold chain and rings, hand-phones, his leather sling bag and even his bloodied clothes had vanished.

But she knew his soul was not at peace. Mo kept appearing in her dreams, standing at the front of the village police station and calling out to her. Sometimes she heard the revving of a lone motorcycle at the porch. She even saw Mo from the corner of her eyes, polishing his motorbike. She remembered riding pillion to work, Mo's strong shoulders blocking the wind. She had weird intuitions that Mo had asked her to cook his favorite food in the mornings. Her son was not dead. Not dead yet. His spirit was restless. *Mo*, she called out, *if you had only listened to Pa. If only I had listened to Pa.* She buried her face in her palms and cried so much that her breasts cramped. *All that milk you suckled, Mo, is now wasted blood.*

On the date commemorating the sixteenth day since Mo's death, Ramesh busied himself preparing for the prayers. But Rukku visited the police station first. She told the officer-in-charge that Mo had been held in the lock up. The puncture marks on his body were bullet holes, and there had been no accident. She told them that she needed to do the prayers at the spot where he died to liberate his soul.

The officer was bewildered. He almost convinced her that her claims were fraudulent with grief before showing her the door. She protested. More officers crowded around her, confused by the event unfolding before them. They told her to stop. They called her a nuisance. They said she was up to no good, a troublemaker like Mo. They said they would arrest her.

Much to their chagrin, Rukku marched out of the station to the corner that housed the lock-up cells. Amid the jeers and mocking, the stocky, mouth-full-of-tongue policeman appeared again. At the top of his voice he shouted, "lezzisbe, lezzisbe." The officer stopped between Rukku and the other frenzied officers, gathered his breath and said, "Let it be." Flustered, Rukku taped Mo's picture on a tree and hung a string of jasmines across it. She spread a banana leaf on the ground. Burning three incense sticks, she laid a bunch of bananas and poked them into one banana. From her bag she produced a coconut, raised a machete and halved it in front of the officers and split it open. She scrutinized its split edges and noticed that it was jagged and not smooth as she had feared. Leaving the halved coconut on the banana leaf, she reluctantly conceded that Mo's passing was fated. She clasped he palms reverently and uttered her prayers. Then she left for home.

How dare they tell me that Mo is bad, she listened to the voice in her head. *How dare they label him useless? How dare they call him a menace? This society, did they not shorten his life with their assumptions? I've seen the money. But illegal substances?* The punctures on his chest and sides remained in her mind, as big as the *pottu* on her forehead, crusted like dried blood. But her protests were muffled. Her hands were twisted and her mouth shut. Ramesh would not come to her aid. The neighbors smirked behind her back. Her relatives blamed her. The policeman asked her to accept the death and let it be.

Rukku wipes her eyes and looks into the cup to find it empty. She catches sight of Mo's motorbike on the side of the porch, covered in a grey tarpaulin sheet. Resentment arises from her guts, creeping up to her head like the allamanda wines. She should have listened to Ramesh. She had laughed at him. Ramesh knew it would take Mo away from them. She gets up and walks toward the motorbike. Ramesh has arrived with the priest and is helping with the arrangements. Mo is smiling down from the wall where his black and white portrait is hanging. A thick garland of roses is hung across his picture, with a smudge of vermillion powder splotched on his forehead.

Rukku quietly pulls off the tarpaulin and pushes the motorbike toward the allamanda bush. She fetches kerosene from the kitchen and pours it all over Mo's motorbike. "It's all because of you," she stutters in anger. A few neighbors have stopped to watch from over their walls. She hurls the empty kerosene container into the thick bush and drives away the roosting birds from their nests. A bystander from the roadside comes to ask what she is up to and calls out to Ramesh. Rukku snubs him angrily and lights a match. In no time, a huge fire engulfs the entire motorbike and the overgrown allamanda.

Ramesh hurries out and pulls Rukku away from the flames. No one tries to extinguish the fire. They stand and watch the motorbike burn, thick black smoke rising toward the sky.

Agitation
by Perry McDaid

Acacia and Albizia brandished verdancy

like foliaged fists

at the past destruction:

a declaration of survival

to a shrugging earth

which had once sloughed

the majesty of Angkor.

Permit for Inle Lake in pannier,

I hugged Mala to me

and bore the good-natured slap –

plus fond displacement –

when my hand strayed

mischievously.

She revved the Kenbo:

preparation for swift crossing

of temporary fix.

I clung in anticipatory terror

much as shirt to my own back

as I assessed the makeshift

ford across the earthquake's breach:

wide fissure to top the cracked-heel

surface of the road.

Quake had made a mockery

of central white lines:

reminder that nature laughs

at our pithy strictures,

each hearty chuckle

bringing more tremors.

The mist seethed from the foliage,

blurring the sky to a powder blue.

Two dead, seventy injured.

Just Run and Run
by William Tham Wai Liang

I stopped on the path up to the mountain, the roaring of Habil's motorcycle engine slowing down to a put-put and gradually growing silent. I tightened the scarf around my neck and warily glanced up at the sky to see the clouds darkening above my head. When it rained the mountain path would turn into a cascade of water and mud, and it would be almost impossible to continue. The air was cold and Cemoro Lawang was still at least half an hour away. A simple brick *warung* stood close by, and I wheeled the Honda toward it, keeping an ear out for the rumble of distant thunder. A man with a few good teeth smiled as I entered.

"From Malaysia?" he asked in a language that was comfortingly familiar but still unnervingly different.

I nodded and looked up. "It might rain."

The *warung* sold iced tea, coffee and fried rice. I had instant white coffee and sipped it, the warmth reassuring in the cool air. The man fiddled with bits of charcoal in a metal box on the floor, trying to light it. "Too wet," he said sadly. "I must let it dry."

I ordered another cup of coffee. The sky brightened somewhat as the clouds began drifting eastward from Java to the Bali Strait. I fumbled in my pocket for change. The bills had strings of zeroes behind them, and I was still having trouble figuring out exactly how much I was paying in ringgit. Meanwhile the owner managed to light a piece, which quickly warmed the *warung* to my appreciation.

"You are going to the volcano?" he asked as I walked out.

"Yes," I said simply.

I had Habil's motorcycle, his jacket and helmet. He was not much bigger than I was, but he was much wilder—stories of the crazy times that he spent in the Jakarta nightclubs punctuating the daily grind of his work at the Company. "Come and visit me in Indo," he often implored over Skype when we managed to fix a time to chat. "It gets very lonely over here."

I finally caught my long-promised flight to the Jakarta airport, exiting into the haze. Habil was casually smoking a cigarette when I arrived with only a backpack, sitting astride his bike. "Welcome!" he said during a massive bear hug. "So glad you could make it."

From the back of the motorcycle I watched as we raced through the haze, bikers in face masks vanishing in and out of the grayness. Jakarta was so big, so massive, that its proportions looked unreal. Where KL still had some semblance of order, this city had none, sprawling in all directions until it reached the sea. I developed a hacking cough, and I could just hear Habil's laughter over the scream of his motorcycle. "You couldn't stay away, could you?" he teased as we veered off the main road into a maze of smaller side streets where clothes hung out to dry from the windows of small slum houses.

"You're very convincing," I said, hoping that he couldn't hear the tremor in my voice.

"So many places to visit in Java. Let's not stay in Jakarta long. It's a great city, but there's so much to see outside of it. I'm on sabbatical and you need a break after your awful marketing job. We can take as long as we like."

He hadn't changed from his student days when we met abroad, fighting off the biting cold of a prairie winter. He had always been urbane, sophisticated and had ditched that distinctive Malaysian accent after a few months in Winnipeg. It had taken me a while to warm up to Habil—behind that slick exterior, he was a ticking bomb ready to implode and collapse on himself. "My dad died of a heart attack. It runs in the family," he said solemnly one night after all of us had been out drinking at the university pub. The air was cold and my lashes were covered with a thin layer of frost, but the bourbon in my stomach kept my cheeks flushed as we trotted to C's place for nachos and late-night Quentin Tarantino movies on somebody's laptop. Everyone mumbled their condolences, and C warned him about his lifestyle. "You're not my mak," he slurred, crossed. "But you are right."

So he continued to burn brightly. That was how I wanted to remember him.

At Cemoro Lawang the sun was already setting. In Java it gets dark by six, and outside of the cities everything shuts down and people drift back to sleep. I nosed my way up the last few yards to the hostel where I had booked a room. My breath emerged in clouds of vapor and my fingers were numb. I wished that I had gloves—it was so easy to forget that the mountains were still cold in the tropics. The lobby was already crowded with foreign tourists speaking in a medley of Dutch and German and French, along with some thick British accents thrown in for good measure. Someone was arguing about the prices. "This is ridiculous!" a woman shouted. "For this price we could stay in Kuta for three days..."

I quit the hostel temporarily, gingerly climbing down the steep slope toward yet another *warung*. The lady in the *jilbab* looked up from behind the counter. I placed my order through the din of voices from the chain-smoking tourists yapping about surfing in Bali. I smiled and answered the usual questions. Yes, I was from Malaysia, and I was traveling alone. "Aren't you nervous?" she asked. "Why aren't you traveling with someone else?"

"We disagreed."

"Ah."

Hot soup for dinner. I wasn't sure exactly what was in it, but I didn't ask. It warmed my insides. The slopes of Bromo were not far away, the mountain spewing clouds of acrid sulfur into the air. I had been checking the warnings frantically over the past few days, worried that they would close off the crater as an eruption seemed likely. But the warnings were soon downgraded and it was *almost* safe to visit the volcano. One of the tourists laughed so loudly and said something in a Malaysian accent. I found myself instinctively turning to take a look at him. It was a habit that I never quite shook off from my Winnipeg days. I was instantly disappointed. He was a scrawny sort of guy with square glasses and a *Cina*-looking face. For a moment I had half-hoped it was Habil. Where was he now? Perhaps he was still in Surabaya having dinner at the Hotel Majapahit, or maybe he had already left for Bali on the ferry from Ketapang as we had planned. After dinner I walked out to the guard post at the entrance to the vast caldera where Bromo and the mountains lay in a vast sea of sand.

"Is it safe to go down now?" I asked the guard, who was wrapped in a thick quilt to keep the cold out.

"Don't stand at the crater for too long," he replied.

On my way back I thought I felt raindrops falling. It was only when I stepped into the light of one of the foyers that I realized it was volcanic ash—a fine dust falling from the sky, borne by the winds from the heart of the earth. For some time I wandered in the darkness.

When I got back to the hostel it was much later at night. In the lobby the jeep drivers who would drive the tourists up to the viewpoints and the slopes of the volcano were chain-smoking and comfortably swaddled in lengths of cloth as I took a seat in front of a panorama of the volcano complex, peering at a paper map and trying to figure out a path down to Bromo. The smell of cloves was strong in the confined space, despite the open doors to let the smoke out.

One of the drivers winked at me as he exhaled a deep breath. "You smoke weed?" he asked.

I shook my head.

His eyes had a faraway quality to them as he lifted the cigarette back to his mouth. "Aceh weed ... Yogyakarta weed ... very good ..."

Outside the air was cold.

That night I tried to remember the details of the trip. How many days had it been? They seemed to pass in a blur. Habil had sped from one place to the next on the motorcycle, chatting about everything, anything. He talked about Jakarta sinking into the sea as we wandered past the Bugis fishing boats at Sunda Kelapa, the harbor stinking of fish. He recited snippets of Indonesian history at Semarang as we wandered past Dutch colonial buildings. At Borobudur I began to roll my eyes as he enthusiastically talked about ancient Buddhist practices while Merapi loomed in the distant horizon. All this while the faithful motorcycle had taken us halfway across the island toward our destination. How long could we go on for? He had a vague plan of finally reaching Flores with its Komodo dragons, hopping from ferry to ferry from one chain of islands to the next, planning out each day on a whim. "You just run and run," I said outside the *kraton* in Yogya, where the Sultan's family resided within.

"My family has a history of heart conditions," he said smoothly. "I might just drop dead tomorrow, darling."

"Please, don't call me that. Ugh!"

"That was exactly what Tiffany used to say."

I couldn't remember which Tiffany it had been: Wong or Hong. Habil's love affairs were drawn out and confusing and, after a while, most of us stopped caring except for C, who kept a running tally. "He probably likes you," C had warned me at one point some years ago, when Habil was busy crying his eyes out over one of the Tiffanies. "Habil is quite a playboy, you know."

"We're just really good friends," I said smoothly, but C was right—it was impossible not to sense Habil's true motivations in our tight-knit circle. So when I bought my ticket for Soekarno-Hatta Airport, I knew exactly what I was getting into. I wasn't quite sure exactly why I did it. Perhaps I genuinely missed his annoying company after our group had gone separate ways. Perhaps it was because we knew we were no longer young. After that magic age of twenty-three when we graduated, the real world beckoned, vast and uncertain and the carefree magic of those student days in the prairies vanished. Habil in particular never grew up. The first chance he got, he accepted a job offer from the Company in Jakarta, trying to prolong his adventures. But running away was useless. There were rumors (spread by C of course) that his mother already had a wife lined up from him, reputedly a relative of one of the royal families.

But by the time we got to Surabaya it was clear that Habil was expecting more than just a travel partner. But he never said anything. I couldn't imagine him being so indirect; half of him was hidden away. "Is there anything you want to tell me?" I asked one evening at the Red Bridge.

"Nah," he lied badly.

The unease had been simmering between us the whole time. It seeped into every conversation and every motorcycle journey, reminding me that we were two very different people suddenly thrust together again. Those few years apart had been enough to turn us into strangers. Sure we could laugh about C and his witty quotes and other misadventures, but all of that was in the past. Sooner or later we had to move on. We both knew that. But of course neither of us said anything. As long as we could pretend that nothing had changed we were fine.

I left before dawn the next morning. Very slowly I rounded the corner and began my journey to the edge of the volcano, the mask on my face keeping out the worst of the sand as the wheels of the bike threw up dust in my wake. The sun rose slowly, but in the near darkness it was just possible to pick out the plume of smoke rising from the crater. The sun continued its ascent; the mountains were soon bathed in a gleaming orange that seemed to jump right out of the photographs I had seen. When at last I brought my bike to a stop at the foot of Bromo, downhill from the steps leading up to its smoking pit, signs of life were showing up. The old Tengger women were setting up their stalls, and a man selling flowers was wandering from the Hindu temple to the top of the mountain. All of this was in the shadow of the immense volcano in the hellish moonscape. I heard a distant neighing and turned toward the edges of the pit. Horsemen were leading their steeds down the farmer trails on the distant sides of the caldera.

I climbed, beginning to cough as the smell of rotting eggs intensified. Habil would have hated being here, out in the face of a terrifying nature far from the cities he had grown up in. Hadn't he complained so much about the prairies, with miles of flat empty land and nowhere to go? No, that had been C, born and bred in KL. Habil was more outdoorsy. Strange how just a few years were enough to erode what I remembered about them. All of us were slowly drifting apart, there was no denying that.

I did not stay there for long. The smoke was thick and blinding and my head was starting to spin. All I did was walk a bit of the way around for some prerequisite photos of the grim surroundings before the stench got to me, and once I was down and away from the pit I sent him a text. *At Bromo now. And what about you?* Not long later he replied. *In Ubud. I will be here a while. Let me know when you get here.*

I tried not to shake. Going back to face him again would be awkward. We had not parted on bad terms. No, it had been so polite and measured that it hurt me to be the one who suggested that we go our separate ways before we rubbed each other raw. "Take the bike," Habil said outside the hostel in Surabaya. "You can ride well enough. Go ahead and head to the volcano. I've been there before anyway."

"But, but..."

"I'll be waiting in Bali," he shrugged. "Take your time."

He seemed relieved at the suggestion, as though he had been thinking about it for days but never voicing what he felt at the back of his mind. "Don't get into too much trouble while you're there, OK?" I warned him a couple of hours later after I was done packing, lifting a leg over the bike.

54

He shrugged. "Aishah's family is pretty big shots. Mak would kill me if I screwed the wedding up with too much ... indiscretion."

"You take care of yourself there, OK?"

"Don't worry about me," Habil replied, alarmed. "Just go. I'll wait for you, and then we'll call it an end. It's about time anyway. Java tends to trap you, it's so big and vast and confusing."

"Always the poet! I'll miss your company, Habil."

He raised a hand in farewell, and almost, as if by accident, he spoke again. "Promise me you'll be there, OK?"

"Promise," I said with a shaky smile as I snapped on the helmet and drove off slowly, joining the rivers of traffic. As I drove down Jalan Sumatera I felt weak. I felt tears in my eyes, and in the rear-view Habil was just standing there, shoulders slumped as I rounded the corner and vanished from the sprawling city and into the countryside on the way to Bromo.

The Vendors
by Khor Hui Min

In my school years, when I hear

Rev of a motorbike as it nears

Signature horn blaring

Excitement triggering

Our favorite treats are here

Ice cream scoops full of cheer

Ice lollies, oh so cooling

All week, impatiently waiting

The bread man with faulty gears

Loud as can be, from far we hear

White fluffy bread, he's bringing

Crackers and sweets, overflowing

Appam man with metal box on rear

Into the box, we eagerly peer

Soft white *appam*, enjoying

Vadai and *putumayam*, delighting

Kuih, kuih! *Kuih* cart is here!

Delicious steamed cakes, we hold dear

Nyonya kuih, happily devouring

Old school stuff, but we are never tiring

For decades, through rain, shine and tears

On the backs of motorbikes, without any fears

Vendors bravely eked out their daily living

Strong and tough, but also kind and forgiving

Down the Rabbit Hole:
Snippets of a Saigon Sojourn
by Don Adams

As I prepared to leave Vietnam after two years of living and working there and return to my job and house and yard and dog and cat and friends and family and life in general in America, I was beset by contradictory emotions. Part of me wanted to run as fast as possible back to that life and wrap myself in it like an old and familiar blanket, as though the whole Saigon sojourn had been a particularly vivid and exhausting dream from which I was about to awaken. And part of me felt like Alice when she refused to go back to her old life (before diving down the rabbit hole) until she was assured of who she would be when she got there. For I was not who I was when I first arrived in Saigon, exuding trepidation. I had become a different person.

Frankly, I needed Vietnam. As I approached the complacency of middle-age living in America, my once inspired youthful enthusiasms were quickly transforming into constraining habits and opinions. I was in real and immediate danger of becoming a blithe sophisticate—that most contemporary of savages, critical of everything and invested in nothing. A typical product of the modern world, I lived my days and nights awash in media as I multitasked away, driven from distraction to distraction. My senses had become too jaded to register anything other than their disturbance, the result being that I was habitually annoyed beyond reason when not bored to tears.

To my credit I was vaguely aware of the dire existential straits I was in. For several years I had been haphazardly trying to goad myself into some sort of deeper awareness. But the various substance-aided alternative regimens of waking and sleeping with which I attempted to disperse the malaise of the quotidian served only to strengthen its spell.

What I was not able to do for myself fate did for me, as I was transported through a series of happy accidents to a far-distant shore with a shockingly unmediated reality.

Eastern mystics tell us that there are three states of human consciousness of reality, which we experience as the worlds of waking, dreaming and dreamless sleep. Each is an illusion, as the juxtaposition of the three readily informs those willing and able to be enlightened. For those of us poor and ignorant souls lost in the *maya* of illusion, however, a further demonstration is in order—as when, exposed to repeated miracles, the unwitting apostles begged of an exasperated Messiah: "We would see a sign."

In Vietnam I was provided with a wealth of signs pointing to the illusory nature of the culturally relative world I had assumed to be objectively real. Indeed one might say that the Western ideal of disinterested objectivity was the first and repeated casualty of my Eastern sojourn.

A more persistent and difficult illusion to dispel was that of the minor myth of myself—the innate belief in the centrality and essentiality of my individual reality—which the alien environment insistently questioned, so that I found myself in the position of a distressed Alice when informed by Tweedledum and Tweedledee that she was merely a sort of something in the Red King's dream: "You know very well you're not real," they told her; or of the starving peasant who protested to his parsimonious lord and master, "I must live somehow," to which his master replied, "I don't see that that is necessary." Must one lose one's life in order to find it? Such, in any case, may be the revelation of a sojourn in a radically alien environment, the startlingly alternative reality of which calls into question all manner of what had hitherto seemed self-evident.

On the other hand, I was going to miss Vietnam awfully. It is true that there were days and times when I had this dizzying and sometimes almost terrifying and sickening feeling that I was floating above the world without one familiar landmark to grab hold of. But for each of those times, there were ten other times when I was literally thrilled to be there, on the crest of a wave that kept cresting.

As I reflected, it seemed to me that these terrifying and thrilling feelings were prompted most often *not* by the serial traumas and dramas that most occupied my conscious attention in my time there, but by casual and random encounters with otherness, to which I responded with instinctive aversion and delight. It would have been unmannerly in the extreme as I prepared to depart to dwell upon the averse, which is in any case quickly forgotten, whereas that which delights has an afterlife as the fondly recalled—anticipating which, in the spirit of a parting gift, I gathered together these random observations of the alternative Vietnamese reality that I had found so diverting and delighting:

I like that the men are not macho and that the women are not coquettes.

I like that the women's traditional "dress" is a trouser set.

I like that one so often sees men walking hand in hand, occasionally even police officers and soldiers.

I like that the Vietnamese police officers wear immaculately tailored and unlikely green-leaf-colored silk uniforms.

I like that the traffic cops ride two to a motorbike.

I like that my students all claimed to keep a diary, which, upon further examination, proved to be a collectively-written "class" diary.

I like that when it is a person's birthday here, he or she pays for everyone else in the party.

I like that hard-up birthday celebrants strive to avoid meeting their well-wishing friends on that very special day.

I like that the gossipy old ladies who gather in the evening across the alley from my house ask the restaurant delivery driver how much the food he is bringing me costs and that he tells them.

I like that people often refer to friends and acquaintances by "number" nicknames. One of my local beer drinking buddies is "Mr. Six."

I like that when I thanked the tipsy owner of the beer stand down the street for buying me a beer, he stuck out his tongue at me.

I like that after a drunken brawl at the beer stand, one of the most vociferous participants came up to me and shamefacedly apologized for the ruckus.

I like that people here often look you right in the eye, to the point of discomfort, and then do not look at you again, as though you don't exist, or perhaps only as an unremarkable piece of the familiar landscape.

I like that I rarely feel that I am being judged in a disapproving fashion by the citizenry simply for being a foreigner and different.

I like that my students are generally thrilled to receive a "C" grade.

I like that the English Department dean insists upon reviewing, amending and approving my course syllabus, and then shows no concern or surprise or interest in the fact that I am not in the least following it.

I like that the English Department and university routinely give me gifts on holidays and special occasions.

I like that the standard of living of English Department professors seems to have no relationship whatsoever to their official university salary. Most of them work as well as teachers and administrators and consultants at private schools—much more remunerative employments made possible by their lowly-paid but highly regarded official university positions.

I like that people are so thrilled when they discover that I know a teensy bit of Vietnamese.

I like that Vietnamese people do not seem to feel obliged to hide their excitement.

I like that people here are rarely self-conscious in public, like the barefoot ball boy at the tennis courts who, having no customers, walked aimlessly around the court, waving his arms in windmill fashion and singing; or like the motorbike taxi drivers on the street corners and sidewalks, who lounge and nap and presumably dream on the back of a motorbike, as though on a couch in their living room. (Their living rooms probably have straw mats and not couches.)

I like that my Vietnamese friends do not seem to take it personally when I complain about the difficulties of living in Vietnam but, on the contrary, good-naturedly join in same.

I like that a perfect stranger who somehow got hold of my phone number was just as politely resigned the tenth time I declined his invitation to coffee as the first time.

I like that there seems to be no truth whatsoever to the guidebooks' assertion that it is impolite to use one's chopsticks to retrieve food from the common bowls of food on the table, which is standard practice even at banquets, just as there seems to be no active taboo against sticking one's chopsticks into a bowl of white rice. When asked about this purported taboo, nobody knows what I am talking about. "You can put your chopsticks wherever you want," a Vietnamese friend assured me.

I like that when I mentioned to a Vietnamese friend that in America it would be considered "unhygienic" for restaurant personnel to be wearing slippers and sandals and that people there almost never go barefoot in public places, as the Vietnamese love to do by kicking off their shoes and sandals when sitting down at offices, restaurants and coffee shops, he replied, "Vietnamese don't care about feet one way or the other. They are not important. They are just vehicles."

I like that the most distinguishing element of the typical Vietnamese physiognomy, at least to my eye, is their cheekbones.

I like that the Vietnamese seem to love their families so much and to hate them too. The same could be said for the country's citizens in general in their emotive relation to one another, particularly in comparison to Americans, who tolerate and fear, rather than love and hate, one another. We don't know each other well enough for that.

I like that the Vietnamese seem always to be eating and yet do not seem particularly concerned with food.

I like that everyone in Vietnam seems obsessed with selling something to everyone else.

I like that, when the police shut down the illegal curbside food and drink stalls on my block, they always and almost immediately reopen.

I like it that the houses in Saigon are so often tall and slender and painted fanciful colors, with elaborate ornamental details on their facades, and that the rooftops of even imposing edifices serve as laundries.

I like that typical Vietnamese walkers neither stride nor stroll, but amble and shuffle, with their feet pointed slightly outward. "The easier to stand up," says my Vietnamese friend—*the easier to change direction*, I think, as I attempt to maneuver around and between their meandering figures with my mono-directional Western stride.

I like that a teenager sitting on his bicycle on the sidewalk near my house was so startled by the sudden apparition of me striding toward him in my purposeful Western manner while on an evening stroll that he instinctively put up his arms as though to ward off a blow.

I like that, on my walks through the neighborhood, adults frequently point me out to children.

I like that it is considered routine in Vietnam to take a two-hour lunch break, complete with nap.

I like that, in most restaurants and wayside eateries, they bring you iced tea gratis or for a nominal charge and that it is a "bottomless" cup.

I like that the Vietnamese word for America may be interpreted "strange flower."

I like that the roaming lottery ticket sellers give me so many chances a day to purchase a ticket.

I like that the buses and freight trucks almost always have someone riding "shotgun" whose main purpose seems to be to lean out of the window and motion to, threaten, scold, intimidate and cajole the motorbike traffic through which the vehicle is attempting to maneuver.

I like that they still have icehouses here that deliver large blocks of ice via truck and motorbike to restaurants and vendors, who then whack at the ice with a sort of mallet to break it into usable pieces.

I like that the sound of ice being whacked is one of the distinctive sounds of Saigon street life, together with the sound of vendors hawking their wares, of noodle delivery boys soliciting orders by beating on a sort of cowbell with a stick and of massage boys (young men) on bicycles who shake a rattle in order to advertise their service.

I like that the young athletes at the sports complex where I swim are so adept at volleyball and badminton and so hopeless at basketball.

I like that even a second-string English soccer player is more famous here than the biggest name football or baseball player in America.

I like that my students who had heard of it thought that Israel was a "Christian" country, "like America," and that when I told them that it was Jewish, they didn't know what that meant--prompting a short lesson on the history of the West.

I like that, when my student on holiday in the countryside fell out of a tall palm tree while retrieving coconuts only to land on a pile of branches and walk away unhurt, the villagers told him that he was the first person to fall out of that tree and live.

I like that, at funerals here, brass and percussion bands play as loudly as they can.

I like that the Vietnamese celebrate death-days more than birthdays.

I like that, while Americans reacted with uniform repulsion when I told them about the rat that got into our house and bit me on the hand while I was sleeping, Vietnamese asked me how it got in and how I killed it.

I like that an American embassy worker in Hanoi was so intimidated by the chaotic traffic that she routinely hired a taxi merely to cross the street.

I like that my preconceived notions of what this world will be like are so entirely wrong and yet so persistent. When we were to take a bus to the countryside, for instance, I could not help imagining an American-style cruiser, whereas we actually rode in a Toyota minivan packed to the gills with passengers. When it became too full to let any more in the door, they passed them in through the windows.

I like that so much of what one does here as a matter of course—such as catching the country-bound Toyota minibus by waiting, like everyone else, with our luggage on the side of the highway—is, strictly speaking, illegal. Which is why, I presume, the bus barely allowed passengers like us to get a foot in the door before speeding off again. Likewise most of the street-side food and beverage stands are illegal, so that it is not at all unusual to have the table and chair one is at removed from before and under one as the police jeep rounds the corner of the street, leaving one standing incongruously on the side of the street holding a bowl of noodles or a glass of iced coffee, attempting to seem natural and inconspicuous.

I like that the Vietnamese do not seem to feel beholden to rules simply because they are the rules.

I like that traveling food peddlers manage to sell fresh and hot food by attaching a bicycle to the back of a food cart, or by pushing it slowly along while loaded with a charcoal burner and/or a hotplate and a battery. One might buy fried eggs with a baguette, stir-fried corn and shrimp, noodle soup, sautéed squid or many other cheap and inventive dishes from these carts. Likewise women carrying large baskets packed with snacks, such as roasted and boiled peanuts and quail eggs, regularly make the rounds of restaurants and beer stands. I am told that most of these traveling snack women come from the poorer, central regions of Vietnam, while the massage boys and old ladies selling lottery tickets generally are from the North.

I like that, when a restaurant or shop is successful, copies of it spring up all around. In the backpacker district, there used to be two side-by-side vegetarian restaurants both claiming to be "The Original Bodhi Tree Restaurant."

I like that highly visible Western brands, such as Aquafina bottled water, have not one but numerous local knock-offs, with slightly different names, but nearly identical packaging and labels.

I like that routine conversational courtesies, such as saying please and thank you, are so often elided in Vietnamese public discourse. To a Westerner, Vietnamese verbal interactions at markets and restaurants etcetera can seem at times alarmingly brusque. For their part, the Vietnamese may well wonder that Westerners so often seem to reserve their most courteous behavior for perfect strangers.

I like that the kids who play in the alley in front of our house refer to me as "Ong My" or "Mr. America."

I like that my friend's relatives in the Mekong Delta were surprised to hear that Americans do not like to eat dog meat.

I like that these same relatives contended with a straight face that the mosquitoes at their farmhouse on the canal next to the rice paddies weren't very bad. I beg to differ. Although I swathed myself in repellant and slept in my clothes under a mosquito net in a stifling hot closed room, I was covered with small welts the next morning.

I like that the trees on each street in Saigon are numbered consecutively with white stencils on their trunks, and that they are watered from tanker trucks throughout the dry season.

I like that city streets are cleaned nightly by armies of workers with homemade brooms made of stiff bristles of branches and limbs latched to long wooden handles.

I like that workers here doing drudgework do not, in general, seem to adopt a drudge-like disposition toward their job.

I like that the group of Vietnamese friends I meet for coffee in the late morning several times each week always find something to talk about and for hours on end. As a courtesy to me these conversations usually begin in English but quickly evolve into fast-paced Vietnamese I am unable to follow, at which point I open my book or notebook and begin to write or read.

I like that their conversation is punctuated by pointed fingers and occasional slappings upside the head and punchings on the arm and is frequently accompanied by laughter. I have just about given up trying to discern when Vietnamese in animated discussions are truly angry and agitated and when they are merely excited and histrionic. I am not certain that they know themselves.

I like that, no matter how earnestly and expertly I might try to mimic the local behavioral motions so as to minimize social discomfort, I still am unable to understand the instinct for Vietnamese social behavior—for why they do what they do as they do it.

I like that when one invites friends to go out socially, one asks them "to drink coffee," whether or not coffee is to be drunk and regardless of whether it is morning or night.

I like that the Vietnamese language is so concrete and un-abstract. My linguist friend here says, "The Vietnamese language loves ambiguity but hates abstraction."

I like that, in verbal disputes, the Vietnamese frequently refuse to listen to one another. Several times when my Vietnamese friend and I have complained about service to waiters or taxi drivers or such, only to receive a barrage of explanation and excuse, and I have asked my Vietnamese friend to translate, he has responded, "I am not listening." I think that this is part of the negotiating culture, and I have found myself doing the same thing. For instance, when a street vendor recently tried to sell me the English-language Bangkok daily for three times the regular price, I said that I would pay twice the Thai price but no more, prompting a long harangue from him, which I instinctively (to my amazement and satisfaction) ignored.

And it worked, because he then gave me the paper for my price without further haggling.

I like that, living in a foreign language environment in which I cannot readily understand verbal discourse, I have learned to distrust language as simple meaning and even to eschew its use. The negotiating culture here contributes to such distrust. When a lottery ticket seller asks one five times in a row to buy a lottery ticket, and one replies in the negative unequivocally each time, only to find the seller still persisting with his entreaties, one naturally comes to distrust the power of words as meaning.

I like that the vast majority of the ex-pats here segregate themselves so earnestly and entirely from the locals, as though instructed to do so.

I like that one's outsider status here gives one so much freedom to observe the extreme artifice of natural social behavior. It is often as though one were at the zoo or watching a documentary on TV (and then suddenly the perspective shifts and it is oneself that is in a cage or box, while everyone else is free to move about as they please, staring with impunity).

I like that my Vietnamese friends are not at all surprised when I change my mind about my plans. In America I feel that I have to explain my vacillations, but here it is not expected.

I like that the Vietnamese use one's given name for both informal and formal addressing—so that I am either "Don" or "Mr. Don." It is like being in a Jane Austen novel.

I like sitting on the side of the street on a miniature plastic stool in the morning, drinking iced coffee and watching the remarkable variety of street-life flowing all around me—the motorbikes with their constant near-accidents, the small-freight trucks running in and out of the nearby warehouses, the vendors and strollers. By contrast I recently visited a new "planned" upper-class residential community development built on the outskirts of the city and there was no street life at all, except for cars headed to and from their garages and gardeners poking at the ornamental turf. The immaculate sidewalks were entirely empty. It was like being in the afterworld with everyone safe in their tombs. "It reminds me of America," I told my friend, who had just purchased a place there. "Yes," she said, "Isn't it wonderful? It is like you are not in Vietnam at all, but in a foreign country. It is so beautiful. There is no other place like it in Vietnam." "There will be," I said.

I like that my eighty-something-year-old friend from the beer stand down the street, who was a French-and-American-trained colonel in the South Vietnamese Army and attended the old elite French high school in Saigon with Cambodia's former King Sihanouk, claims to care nothing about politics but to be interested only in drinking beer and reading French and English novels. I have given him several of the latter and also a three-volume copy of Gibbon's *Decline and Fall of the Roman Empire* that I lugged over here and read—presented with which, he said to me, "That will take me a while to finish." Then he asked me to write an inscription in it and said, "Please make it as long as possible."

I like that I have found in Vietnam not so much answers to questions, as questions that I had never thought of asking.

Point of Departure
by Thomas De Angelo

"Why do you even bother?" Rozmi Kontum asked his mother as she stood knee-deep in water.

The floodwaters in the house had reached the same level as outside on the streets. Even though the rushing water subsided a day ago the damage was already done. It happened often during rainy season, like a recurring bad dream. Even now the Malaysian sun hung weakly behind a patch of clouds leaving a yellowish tint on the stagnant water in the holes along the road. Rozmi's eyes shifted to the window where he could see the ixoras that his mother and some of the neighbors planted as hedges. They were now broken and squashed by the rains. He and his friends, when they were young, used to suck the sweet nectar out of the plant. Rozmi thought to himself that they would only be sucking mud now.

"I bother because it is our home," his mother answered, as if to herself. Her voice held a mixture of defiance and disappointment.

"It is time you started thinking about your own future. Why don't you ask that girl Ainon to marry you and settle down?"

"Settle down to what? A life without a job, without a chance?"

"Don't you think I know how you earn your money? You and your gang are nothing but losers." She bit her lip to hold back the tears.

"Compared to who? To my father who drank himself to death? To you who works as a maid and cleans other people's dirt. For what? To live in this hole?"

"I told you, it is our home," she answered, gaining her composure.

"This place is a mess. It will always be a mess," Rozmi said, reaching for the keys of his Yamaha YZF-R125 motorbike, which he kept on a nail over the front door. He stole the bike from an American he sent to the hospital after knocking him off a dark road. The man had left the bike to urinate and Rozmi just happened to be at the right place at the right time. He was still high from the methamphetamines he and his *mat rempit* riders took when they were racing. The American was a few feet behind the Yamaha when Rozmi slammed into him with his old bike. He hid the Yamaha for six months before selling his old bike. Now it was his prized possession. He figured he could get at least 7,000 US dollars for it. Not that he had any intention of selling it.

"Where are you going?" his mother asked, already knowing the answer.

"Where I always go."

"Why?"

"Because I'm bored, and there is nothing else to do," Rozmi answered.

"And you think that *mat rempit* gang is your answer?"

"My answer is the motorbike I sit on the back of—when I drive and try to leave all this behind."

"You won't be driving in water. It isn't a boat."

"I parked it in a garage on Lorong Pudu. You know that."

"Can't you stay off that bike for one night?"

"Not even for one minute," Rozmi answered, already thinking of what tricks he would do on the stretch of uncompleted road along the coast. He had been practicing the Superman where he drove lying flat on the seat. He hoped Ainon would be there to watch. She didn't approve, but she came all the same.

"You and your friends are nothing but criminals," she yelled through the open window.

Rozmi waded through the water clutching the keys to his motorbike in his hand as if it were some lucky amulet that would save him from all this.

His mother was right, he thought to himself. They were only criminals, but that was the purpose. As if to get even with a world that offered them no opportunities; they didn't care about racing as much as they did about being a nuisance, a thorn in the side of authority.

The water began to drop below his knees and then his ankles. Soon he was on dry land. He decided not to go back home after racing. There no longer seemed to be any point. Besides, he needed gas money, so he would have to snatch a tourist's purse when he reached Brickfields. Some tourist would be staring up at the skyscrapers after checking into one of the posh hotels and not even notice when he stepped behind her and grabbed her purse. That, too, was getting boring, but he decided long ago to let the migrants do the work. He would use his brain. The rich tourists didn't deserve what they had anyway. He needed gas and someone had to pay.

Rozmi retrieved his motorbike and made his way toward Jalan Petaling. He could see Ainon as he approached the street. Most of the gang were there, and he noticed Umar standing next to Ainon. Umar was the one member he couldn't take to. His arrogant attitude and the way he always flirted with Ainon gave Rozmi a desire to run him off the road if he ever had a chance. The street was already a crowded conglomeration of tourists, locals, drug dealers and prostitutes. The gang met here to buy the methamphetamines before hitting the road. When the others noticed him slow down, they all put their helmets on and got on back of their bikes. Once the helmets were on, they all felt invisible as well as invincible. Another member, Bakri, pulled alongside Rozmi and passed him a handful of pills. Rozmi took one and stashed the rest in his pocket. He moved closer toward Ainon. Umar turned, pretending he didn't see Rozmi, and put on his helmet as he got on his bike. Ainon smiled and gave Rozmi a look as if to say 'don't worry about him. I can handle him.' Rozmi returned a look that seemed to say 'I don't care.' When Rozmi caught Umar's eyes, his expression changed and conveyed silently the words 'touch her and I'll kill you.'

Ainon walked toward Rozmi's bike. He took off his helmet.

"Don't race tonight, Rozmi," Ainon said, in the form of a plea.

"I have to."

"Why?"

"They expect me to."

"I had a dream that you would be hurt," she said, knowing her words would seem childish to him.

"I don't care about dreams. I need to ride with them. It's what we do."

"You do what your gang wants and not me," Ainon said, her voice full of anxiety.

"I need their respect."

"Why don't you leave this gang? You could sell the bike. We could go away. Maybe to Singapore."

"And then what?" Rozmi said, reaching into his pocket and taking another pill.

"I don't know. Get real jobs. Settle down. Maybe get married."

"You sound like my mother," Rozmi said, revving the engine.

Rozmi's *mat rempit* gang sped across town toward an unfinished stretch of land alongside a construction site where they would do their stunts. A grocer poked his head out of one of the shops and yelled at them as they went by.

"Stop with this noise. You should all get jobs and stop this nonsense."

Rozmi slowed down first, followed by Bakri and then the rest. They stopped their bikes and stared at the grocer. One of the gang got off his bike and, within a few seconds, took out a small club and hit the grocer across the face. The man fell with a thud as blood gushed from the open wound. Without a word the gang started up and drove away. The typical night had begun.

Rozmi noticed Ainon driving in a car with some girlfriends. They were following the gang and witnessed what happened to the grocer. Rozmi detected a few tears on Ainon's face. He reached into his pocket and took out another pill, which he swallowed as he accelerated his bike.

It was dusk when they arrived at the place where they would do their stunts. A crowd had already gathered. Ainon and her friends, as well as similar groups of girls, were scattered about the outskirts of the dirt track. The *mat rempit* gang parked their bikes in a circle and began mingling with the crowd, boasting of the tricks they would be performing. They all continued to pop methamphetamines. Some of them drank a mixture of palm wine and turtle blood that they called 'fearless water' while others took whatever drugs they were given.

Ainon walked over to Rozmi.

"Please, Rozmi, just tonight. For me. Let's get out of here. You can always ride tomorrow."

"What's different about tomorrow?"

Umar walked up, more arrogant then ever and obviously very high.

"What's the matter, Ainon? You finally tired of him?"

Rozmi turned the key and started the ignition.

"I'm going. I'll finish with you later, Umar."

Ainon grabbed Rozmi's arm.

"But what about me?"

"I'll do the first trick for you," Rozmi said, driving toward the other riders.

They were all on their bikes. Umar was last to join them.

"Let's do a few races. Then we can do our tricks one at a time," Rozmi suggested.

"What about you and I race first?" Umar said, still arrogant and still high on pills.

Rozmi took a pause and eyed Umar. In a flat-toned voice he said, "Let's go." He revved the engine and drove to the makeshift starting gate.

Umar hesitated a second and then followed.

At the gate they waited for the signal to begin. Rozmi was already concentrating on how he intended to run Umar off the road. There was a concrete barrier beyond which was a forty-foot drop into a pile of stones. Rozmi wondered if he could run Umar into the concrete and possibly right off the embankment.

Dabbing her eyes, Ainon stood on the sidelines with an anxious expression on her face. The signal was given, and Rozmi took the lead immediately. He knew he was certain to win and decided to forego his original plan of running Umar off the road. Instead he would beat him handily and impress Ainon while at the same time humiliating Umar. He would choose another time to destroy Umar.

Rozmi wheeled his bike to where Ainon stood so he could watch the remaining races with her. Then the tricks and stunts would begin.

"I made Umar look like an idiot, didn't I?" Rozmi asked Ainon.

"I guess. Can we leave now?"

"Leave?"

"Yes. I told you I was afraid for you to race tonight. Well you did, and I'm glad nothing happened and it's over. Why don't we get something to eat and go back to my apartment? All my roommates are here. We'll have the place to ourselves."

"I can't leave now. We still have our tricks. People are still arriving to watch."

"Rozmi, I don't think I can go through this anymore. We see riders dying every day. It's just a matter of time for you too."

"So what?"

"How can you say that? We can have a future."

"I'm not selling the bike. This is what I am."

A loud crash interrupted their talk. They turned and saw two *rempits* limping off the road. Their bikes were lying off the track in a twisted clump of metal.

"They're all right," Rozmi said.

"See what I mean? Just a matter of time."

"We'll see. I have to go now. I'm doing the Superman, and I'm going to try the Scorpion as well."

"One trick is dangerous enough. Isn't the Scorpion the one where you stand on the seat with one leg and do a wheelie?"

"Yeah."

"Are you trying to kill yourself?"

Rozmi laughed and took another pill from his pocket. "I'm going. If you still want to go back to your apartment, I'll see you later."

Ainon tried to answer, but her voice was drowned out by the roar of Rozmi's motorbike. She joined her girlfriends who were talking to a group of new riders who just arrived. The crash temporarily ended the racing and now the tricks and stunts were beginning. Rozmi was up first, but Ainon couldn't watch. She turned her back and asked a friend to tell her what happened.

"He's lying flat on his seat doing the Superman, and he must be going 100 miles an hour.

Ainon felt her heart racing and wondered how long she could wait for Rozmi to change.

"He's done. Another rider is getting set to ride."

Ainon turned back to watch and moved closer to the track to try and signal Rozmi to take her home. Umar walked his bike to where she stood.

"Why don't you give up on him and come with me?" Umar asked, putting his hand out.

Ainon ignored him. He moved next to her.

"Come on," he said, touching her face with his fingers.

"Leave me alone, Umar," she said, and walked toward an area away from the track and near the embankment where the crowd had thinned out and she could breathe some air.

Umar followed her, still on his bike. Rozmi was moving toward them on his bike, going slowly as he scanned the crowd for Ainon. He spotted her and quickened his pace. As he drew closer he could see Umar standing next to Ainon. Umar was still on his bike.

"Let's go, Ainon," Umar said, reaching out and attempting to touch her breast.

Rozmi saw it all and accelerated. He decided in a split second to ram into Umar's bike and push him off the road. If he timed it correctly he figured he could drive him right over the edge of the embankment.

Umar tried to touch Ainon again. She pushed him away. Just as Rozmi accelerated at full speed Umar leaned to the side to grab Ainon and moved out of Rozmi's path. It was too late for Rozmi to stop. He hit the tip of Umar's bike and the impact spun him out of control. The front of his bike struck a concrete divider and propelled him over the embankment. Rozmi's motorbike hit the stones hard and within a few seconds the bike burst into flames.

It took an hour for the police to reach the spot and extinguish the flames. A stretcher with Rozmi's body on it was pulled up with ropes. The bike itself was towed up with a winch and chain. Smoke still could be seen coming off the metal. Ainon's girlfriends tried to hold her back, but she pushed through just as the ambulance sped away. She reached the spot where the bike was being dragged onto a truck and, as she got there, the keys fell out of the ignition. She picked them up. They were still hot. She held them tightly in the palm of her hand when she was driven home. She gripped them harder until it hurt. The pain was already moving from her palm to her heart where it would remain. It would resurface every time she saw someone on the back of a motorbike or heard the roar of an engine.

Accident
by Gillian Craig

It may have occurred to us,

in that unusual crush of traffic

early on a Hanoi Saturday

along the dyke road.

Yet it was still gut twisting

to see an awkward truck,

left side smashed and crumpled,

indicating a white car

with a red-splashed

thump on the driver's side,

and much worse, the shattered

motorbike in a pooling bruise.

The audience made statements.

Lowered eyes caught two bouquets

of incense, writhing, fuming

on the detached saddle.

An entreaty to move on,

and not haunt this place,

causing further harm

through spite and vengeance.

An entreaty to move along,

not cause more damage,

as if the living were all blameless

and the dead had started this.

And so it goes. And so it goes.

The witnesses cross lanes,

steering into oncoming traffic

to avoid that stain, that fate.

Casta Diva
by Daniel Emlyn-Jones

Brother Columba of the missionary school in Kuching put the needle to the record, and from the crackling machine there arose a voice unlike any I had ever heard before. Everything outside—the kempt school garden of palms and bougainvillea stretching down to the road and beyond it through the haze of heat and sultry air to the distant Sarawak Club— faded into unreality. I fought back tears. The voice of the singer was visceral, like the cry of an animal, luminous as burnished gold. When the piece was finished, Brother Columba beamed as he laid a hand on my shoulder. "It's alright Thomas. You are not the first person to cry after hearing Joan Sutherland's interpretation of 'Casta Diva'."

From that afternoon onward, I tried to sing as I had heard Joan Sutherland sing. Although with my boy soprano voice I could hit the high notes, I knew I was a very poor imitation indeed of the great singer. Around this time I remember my father caught me in my bedroom with one of my sister's shawls around my head, pretending to be the priestess Norma.

"What you doing?" His face was twisted in a look of irritated bewilderment.

"Practicing."

"Practicing what? To scare away the birds?"

Though my father and mother were mystified by my new hobby, I knew they approved of my afterschool meetings with Brother Columba. Irish by descent, he had traveled to the community from Rome some years before and had brought with him an air of foreign sophistication to the relatively small Kuching Catholic community. Those who had hosted him for tea on a Sunday afternoon wore the fact like a badge of distinction. Both my mother and father seemed to think he must be grooming me for the priesthood, every parent's dream for their second son.

Over the weeks with Brother Columba, I steadily listened to his entire record collection: Wagner, Bellini, Donizetti, Mozart, Beethoven, Rossini and Weber. He would tell me about the lives of the composers, the stories the arias were expressing and the careers of the singers who were interpreting them. He would study my face as I listened and afterward would ask me what I thought. It was the first time in my life anyone had asked me what I thought about anything. The meetings quickly became the highlight of my day, and I'd look forward to the next one shortly after the previous one was over. Eventually, I summoned the courage to ask Brother Columba the question that had been on my mind for some time: "Will you teach me to sing?"

He rested back in his chair and sighed deeply, as he did when confronted with any question, ranging from the nature of God to whether he wanted a cup of tea. "I have no experience," he replied. "Training the voice is a great art."

"But you'll be better than having no teacher at all." I offered.

"An incompetent teacher can be worse than not having one ... but perhaps you have a point." He got up from his seat and took me through to the church where he sat at the old Bechstein and began playing a hymn, nodding for me to join in. I sang hesitantly at first, but with his encouragement and the way my voice echoed in the big space, I gained in confidence.

"Very good!" he exclaimed when we had finished. "Not bad at all."

I grinned from ear to ear.

"We have to get you singing at mass!"

I gaped. "Solo?"

He nodded.

"But I can't."

"Of course you can!" He fixed his large brown eyes on me. They were kind but with a perpetual ironic twinkle. "Fear is a phantom. It is a voice in our head that we have the power to silence."

My first performance at mass was Schubert's "Ave Maria" during the communion. I was shaking as the organ began the accompaniment, but once I began to sing and heard my voice—pure and clear, echoing around the church—it became the most exciting experience of my life. I saw my mother and father in the communion queue, jolted from their pre-communion prayers to glance up at the organ loft in disbelief. After that Sunday I became a regular performer at mass, and the whole community began to talk of my talent. My mother bathed in the admiration and envy of the other women. My father, on the other hand, seemed quite embarrassed by the whole thing.

As the months went by, I realized that singing was what I wanted to do with my life. When I broached the subject with Brother Columba, he flinched. "It's a wonderful thing to want to pursue, but the music business is tough, and there's no guarantee of success. The great singers we've listened to spent many years working and struggling. You also have to consider that your voice has not broken yet. You have a beautiful voice now, but who knows what your adult voice will be like. And there is no music school in Sarawak. You'd have to travel abroad to study."

"But it's what I want to do. Anything else seems like a waste."

When I looked at Brother Columba, I saw tears shining in his eyes.

"No!" was my father's response when I asked him at dinner. He waved his chopsticks in the air, oblivious to the fragments of rice which went flying across the room to the wincing and scowling of my mother. "Sing at mass. Fine. But you need to think of your rice bowl. When you are a man, you'll need money. Where are you going to get it from? From me? I can't feed you forever."

"Singers get paid," I replied.

My father laid his chopsticks on the table and pointed a finger at me. "I don't know a single singer who gets paid. You don't get paid to sing at mass. Mr. Kuek sings when he cooks *char kway teow*, but he doesn't get paid. My mother's cousin used to sing in a bar for white men after the war. She got paid, but believe me, she did more than just sing."

"In other countries, singers get paid to sing opera."

My father laughed. "Ah, so now you're a twelve-year-old boy who wants to go to the other side of the world to learn opera. You must be re-a-lis-tic." He jabbed his finger forward at each syllable of the word, as if hammering a nail.

"When I'm older I could."

"And who's going to pay?"

I was silent.

"You don't think of these things, you see? You're day dreaming." He shrugged and went back to eating.

I looked at the food on my plate and suddenly had an urge to throw it in my father's face.

"Have you ever thought of the priesthood?" he said, his tone suddenly warm and encouraging. "That's a good thing to do. You'd get to sing at mass as much as you wanted if you were a priest."

"But you have to be called by God," I said.

"Maybe you are being called by God, but you're just not listening. Have you spoken to your friend, Brother Columba, about it? Perhaps he can help you to listen?"

It was after Holy Week 1967—when I had turned thirteen—that Brother Columba showed me a clipping from a Singaporean newspaper. Auditions were being held in June for places at the Bidwell Music School in Singapore. Scholarships were available, and if I succeeded, I would study music alongside the other subjects.

"I want to go," I said immediately. I knew it would be difficult to leave my mother and my sisters, but by then my desire for music was stronger than anything else.

"We will need your parents' consent."

"My father won't."

Brother Columba sighed. "We'll see."

The following Sunday afternoon, my little sister suddenly came running into the kitchen. "Br Br Brother Columba!" she shouted. My mother yanked a curtain and glanced out the window to see him ambling down the lane toward the house, his gait swaying like a ship in a squall. Like lightening she circled the sitting room, wiping debris from tables and chairs, and pushing children outside. She arranged a throne-like wooden chair for the Brother; it had been on the junk ship which brought the family from Fujian in 1862 and was almost as revered as he was. My father, still wearing his Sunday best, visibly straightened and pulled at his cuffs.

Brother Columba drifted genially in and nodded to everyone. "I realized the other day that I have never visited you good people, stalwarts of St. Aloysius though you are. How very remiss of me."

"Not at all," replied my mother. "You are a very busy man, and we're delighted to welcome you now. Would you care for a cup of tea, Brother?" She was speaking in her best English, slow and robotic and quite funny to listen to.

"Thank you. That would be delightful."

While my mother was preparing tea, Brother Columba turned to my father. "Mr. Liu, what a fine house and gardens you have here."

"Believe me, Brother, every brick and every square foot I have paid for with sweat and blood."

Brother Columba bowed to him. "Indeed. You are a credit to your church, your community and to your family."

"I have had no choice, Brother. We work or we starve."

"And how is business?"

"Not too bad. Sometimes good, sometimes slow, but it never dries up. Builders will always be needed in Kuching."

My mother returned to the living room and handed Brother Columba a cup of jasmine tea from a prized, fine-bone china set that rarely came down from a high shelf in the kitchen cabinet. The Brother sipped from the delicate little cup, sighed and leaned back in his chair. It was as if he were attempting to radiate serenity throughout the entire room. "I must confess that my dropping by this afternoon is more than just a social visit."

"Ah," said my father.

Brother Columba then told my parents about the Bidwell Music School and the idea of me auditioning for it.

"It's very good of you, but we must say no," said my father.

"It is, of course, completely up to you, but it would be a wonderful opportunity for Thomas."

"With respect, Brother, you haven't thought it through. Even if Thomas got the scholarship, who will pay for the flight to Singapore? I don't have that kind of money to spare."

"I have some funds that could be used," replied Brother Columba.

"No, I'm sorry, Brother. It's very kind of you to think of Thomas in this way, but it's not possible. He belongs here in Kuching with us. We need him to help out with the business during the holidays. Going off to Singapore just wouldn't work."

Brother Columba sighed and nodded.

"I was wondering, though, Brother," said my father in his shrewd voice, "if Thomas might be suitable for the priesthood?"

"It is always possible, but a vocation must come from God and can only be confirmed through a long period of prayerful discernment."

"Ah, and maybe God is calling Thomas?"

"God calls us all to many different vocations. You and your wife have a vocation as parents, I have a vocation as a Christian Brother, and I believe your son is being called to be a musician."

"Ah yes, Brother. There are vocations and then there are dreams. We all have dreams. I wanted to be president when I was Thomas' age!" He guffawed loudly.

After some more small talk, Brother Columba heaved himself out of his chair, thanked my parents for the tea, and my mother walked him back through the front garden to the road.

I spent the afternoon in my room crying. My mother eventually came to call me to dinner. "What's the matter?" she asked, though she knew the answer.

"I want to be a musician," I sobbed.

She sat on the edge of my bed and smoothed my hair with her hand. "If you want to be a musician, you will be a musician."

"But father will never say yes, and he's the head of the family."

"You mustn't underestimate me, Thomas," she said gently. "Remember that your father and I have been married for twenty years. He may be the head of the family, but sometimes the wife can be like the neck and tell the head which way to turn."

Ten minutes later, I heard shouting downstairs. My mother let my father have the last word on almost everything, but when on rare occasions she refused to go along with him, it was a sight to behold. I crept downstairs and poked my head around a corner to get a good view.

"You think just because you had no opportunities when you were a child, your children shouldn't have any opportunities either?" She gesticulated furiously as she spoke, her eyes aflame. "It's different nowadays. Mrs. Wong's son is studying computers. Mrs. Law's son is going to apply to be a doctor. Mrs. Chang's daughter wants to be a lawyer." She exaggeratedly counted the examples on her fingers in front of her husband. "Thomas has an opportunity to study at a brilliant school in Singapore, but it won't just be music. He'll study all the other subjects as well: math, science, computers, Chinese and history. But you don't want any of that!" She threw her arms violently up in the air, as if casting off a cobweb which had been bothering her for months.

My father had adopted a posture I hardly ever saw, his hands not pointing or thumping, but down and spread, as if in supplication."But Ah Huay ..."

"No!" she snapped. "I tell you. If you don't sign that form and give our son this opportunity, by all the saints, I'll make your life a living hell!"

The next morning, my mother handed me the form signed by her and my father. I took it to Brother Columba after school. He beamed at the piece of paper, as if my father's consent was something inevitable that merely required patience and prayer.

"We'd better get our air tickets now, hadn't we?" he said.

"I thought that religious brothers weren't allowed their own money?" This point had puzzled me since Brother Columba made the offer.

"We aren't," he said with a grin. He then took me outside to a shed at the bottom of the school grounds, an unremarkable building that I had always ignored. He unlocked the padlock and opened the door.

"Some dreams, like yours, are meant to be," he said. "Some are not."

I poked my head through the doorway and peered into the darkness. I could smell oil and leather upholstery, and noticed a glint of metal. Once my eyes had adjusted to the darkness, I gaped in shock. Before me was a brand new Harley Davidson motorbike: writhing silver engine pipes, polished red mudguards and an exhaust system that looked as if it could breathe fire. If there was an object in this universe that was least likely to be associated with Brother Columba, it was standing there in that old shed.

He enjoyed my look of shock. "It was a youthful infatuation. I've had a buyer for some time, but until now I've never felt like parting with it. Sentimentality, I suppose." Without thinking, I flung my arms around him.

We meticulously prepared my audition pieces, and before I knew it, the day we would travel to Singapore for my audition had already come. In the end I was accepted at the Bidwell School of Music and spent six happy years there. My voice broke when I was fourteen, but fortunately my adult voice turned out to be a vibrant tenor. I had a reasonably successful career with the Singapore Lyric Opera. In my fifties, I settled back in Kuching to be close to my mother, who by then had been widowed. It was then that I founded Kuching's first music school.

Whenever I traveled back to Kuching during my years abroad, I always paid a special visit to Brother Columba and the room where it had all started. He died at the age of ninety-two in his sleep—as serene in death as in life—and I sang at his funeral. I will always be gratefully to him for opening my heart to music and will never forget how he first sent me to music school in Singapore using the profits from the sale of his Harley Davidson motorbike.

Rohan and Jui Liat
by Ling Tan

KUALA LUMPUR

It starts with soup:

A cauldron compounded of

dongquai and red jujube

Which she drinks once a month

A tonic for her female wiles.

Fueled by *tongkat ali*

He dreams of flying

A wound catapult sailing through the air:

The cruise of a joyous crescendo,

The coast of an inevitable crash: nature loading its dice.

"Merdeka! Merdeka! Merdeka!"

Three times the call is issued;

Three times echoed multitudinously.

Malay, Chinese, Indian

A triangle of imported interests.

Gyring to coalescence:

In the year nineteen hundred and fifty-seven,

(At the tail end of the Baby Boom)

That thirty-first day of August,

The birth of a nation, in the middle,

Splitting those of Rohan and Jui Liat: June/Dec.

(His Gemini to her Sagittarius, the Virgin between them.)

The first time ever they lay eyes on each other,

Is the night a city goes amuck.

That fateful thirteenth of May, 'sixty-nine,

The outbreak of race riots.

 Is not twelve a coming-of-age? A feast of fires?

She was the girl who came to do her homework and stayed to play.

Jui Liat, the school friend of his sister, Aziza.

Also the student of his father, the *munshi*.

A Chow Kit girl in Kampung Baru

In the throng of the mob brewing at the house of a big shot.

She had had to be concealed by the family. Stayed overnight.

How, at the break of dawn, he'd had to walk her to Campbell Road

To a portico where, shaded by a pillar, with Rohan keeping watch,

Behind his back, Jui Liat lifted her arms in a strip tease predicated on the

shedding of *baju* and *sarong* (borrowed from his sib)

To be revealed in the tie-dye blouse and bell-bottoms of her own creation.

Once, for the briefest second, glances are crossed

At the Odeon Theatre on School Concession Day;

Romeo and Juliet on the big screen,

Shakespeare and on the Eng Lit syllabus, making it a must-see for all

secondary schoolboys and girls,

Olivia Hussey and Leonard Whiting, *alamak*, so very cool.

The next time Fate throws them together

Is in the umbrous vales of the Pantai campus, University of Malaya.

Assigned, for orientation, to the same residential college, the Fifth,

Jui Liat and Rohan sitting together in the cafeteria

Splitting a conspiratorial cigarette.

She rises to the Economics Faculty,

(Whereat much is made of the NEP, New Economic Policy.)

He is a science super-freshie.

Hand to hand in palmer's kiss, late nights in the main library together, they

study.

Flirting outrageously to stay within the bounds of friendship.

Love is *halal* lunching on fishballs sold by the *yong tau fu* man from the

back of a motorcycle.

Unwilling to trust the polar opposite, each,

It comes to nothing.

She fence-sits. Hems and haws. What good could come of asking for it?

About her, delicately, he smells the pork. It keeps him at bay.

So close, yet so far.

One night, on the verge of finals fever,

(The night at the Paramount, *Saturday Night Fever* playing, John Travolta

strutting on the disco floor, *aiya,* those hips, those lips, so, so very hot)

Rohan and Jui Liat kissing in the dark. Making out in the cosmic cut.

The morning after, falling over each other with unspoken apology.

The divide is so great they may as well not be in the same land.

The day is hot, the caplets abroad. The night is young, the moon in its full

monty.

The year of work following graduation

Is honed to the mutual tending of a scholarship application.

He pulls off the incredible: a Rhodes on the heels of his first class honors.

She inveigles a grant to Hawai'i.

Paths divergent, they become dead to each other.

NEW YORK

"Rohan ..."

"Jui Liat ..."

"What in heaven's name ..."

"... are you doing here at the consulate?"

Into each other's arms, they swoon: cocooned.

How is it possible?

That fey synchronicity of old

Falling, just like that, into groove.

The two of them getting a new passport concurrently,

How is it conceivable?

And she there only for two weeks, how freaky.

Primarily to attend her daughter's graduation from Sarah Lawrence,

At the same time profiting from the timing to benefit from the services of a consulate.

In highland Guatemala, she lives, on the shores of magical, mystical Lake Atitlan.

Foodie, clean-eater, artist, practitioner of the healing arts, seer, crone,

A yogi on MWF, *qigong* on Tues, Bhajans at New Moon and Full.

He takes her to Muafakat,

This hip new restaurant in the East Village

That he just happens to own.

Undulating her lips around the quadra-syllable —

Suggestive, erotic –

She is disarmed.

Consensus is, well, consensual.

Muafakat is a song playing in her head in all its multitudinous variations.

It starts with soup:

All of it *umami*.

Whether

 Bittersweet or hot and sour;

Bone broth chock full of glutamine,

Extract of *tongkat ali*,

Decoctions of *dongquai* and red jujube slow-simmered in a double vessel,

Fortified with shitake or miso,

The gold of turmeric its antibacterial seal,

Garlic twinned with star anise in a braise of soy sauce,

Coconut milk laced with screwpine (embraced by chia)

Sambals redolent with shrimp paste,

Antioxidant, detoxifying, carotenoid, tonic, aphrodisiac: alchemical all.

Triggering the gates that flood the system: serotonin chased with dopamine.

Deadly infallible.

Indefatigable,

A primal brew deft with budding promise.

What's in a name?

Everything.

In Between
by Pauline Fernandez

After a day of rain—a typical June morning in Quezon City—the humidity caused a thin sheet of sweat to form across my back underneath my coarse, plaid dress. I did not particularly want to wear that thick dress, especially not since my youngest sister, Sonia, was wearing the exact same dress, hers slightly smaller in size, of course.

"But you guys match!" my mother had said, excitedly. "Don't you want that?"

Not really, but Sonia couldn't care less. There wasn't really anything really wrong with the blue and gray plaid dress other than the fact that she had the very same one on. True, it was a little coarse and much too warm to wear in such weather. Too warm to wear for any weather in the Philippines for that matter. But it came from the U.S., and that was all that really mattered. Never mind that it was my American-born cousin's former elementary school uniform. Who cared? No one else in the Philippines knew that. No one had ever seen pictures of her and her thirty classmates wearing the exact same dress. My mother thought it was more than good enough.

We were primped and prepared, polished and clipped to the best of my mother's ability. I was not to move around too much—no jumping nor swinging around like usual, lest I expose my underwear for everyone to see. Feeling pretty as I did, I was willing to comply but knew that restlessness would eventually set in and that in a matter of hours, all that primping and polishing would have gone to waste.

I slipped into my shiny, black school shoes, walked through my father's clinic where his instruments were piled in long, metal boxes on the counter next to the bony, metal operating table and then passed through his home office. I joined the rest of the family—my father, three other sisters and brother—on our driveway as they packed themselves into our little, red, two-door coup hatchback. I would've rather we took my father's old, bronze jeep. It wasn't that much bigger, but the plastic tarp ceiling and the lack of doors and windows at least allowed enough air inside, unlike the stifling coup. But, unfortunately, my parents insisted on the so-called more proper-looking hatchback. I squeezed myself into the back to join my siblings, all five of us jammed together.

"In and out, everyone. In and out," my mother announced as she set herself on the passenger seat, settling my youngest sister on her lap.

From the backseat, we alternately moved our rear ends forward and back, supposedly to make more room as my mother had theorized. It didn't make much difference, but the idea behind it gave us some comfort.

And then we were off. We were supposed to join a family for lunch, an acquaintance of my father, another one of his patients. I don't recall ever meeting them.

We drove through the same narrow, jagged streets streets we go through everyday—to school, the malls, the grocery store, church, my grandparents. In time we began to make our way further into the city, to areas we rarely ventured to. It was drab and gray in the daytime, tired and dotted with people, traffic and squatter homes. But at night, it drapes itself in a cover of darkness, slipping into a flashy string of moving neon lights, luring and selling itself to passerbys. Either way—morning or night— curiosity often had me staring at it. My siblings must have felt the same.

Aside from the small talk between my parents in the front seats, the backseat was completely silent with all of us staring out the windows as traffic buzzed by with a hum. I leaned my head against my older sister's shoulder, my eyes shutting for what was meant to be a brief moment. But I awoke to a strange smell—an unpleasant sweetness mingled with the acrid scent of burnt rubber.

I lifted my head off of my sister's shoulder and turned to look out the car window. I didn't quite know where we were or how we got there. Outside, the heavy gray skies seemed to fuse with the equally dark gray hills beneath. Except they weren't exactly gray. Upon closer look, the hills were not of solid ground, but of broken pieces of everything—plastic bags, paper, cartons, different things of different tints and shades, piled and crushed so close together that the individual colors were no longer distinguishable, but melded into gray.

The Smokey Mountains. So this was what the place looked and smelled like. I'd seen it and heard about it so many times—at school, on TV and at church. Someone always asked for donations. It wasn't the same pretty Smoky Mountains like in that American song about being on top of old Smoky. It wasn't made of forests and nature. It was smoke and trash, a vast landfill where Manila dumped all of its forgotten and broken things.

Red light and the car stopped. I turned and noticed movement among the hills. Men, a few women and children were scattered about, hunched over and going through the same motions of picking out pieces, discarding them and then picking another. I would've missed them had we not stopped. Their drab skin and clothes nearly blended into the hills.

The elevated concrete walls that held the piles together were barely visible behind the stained, mismatching wooden slats, metal tins and wispy cloths of curtains of the squatter huts that lined the sidewalks. Street vendors wandered from the sidewalks into the streets in between the waiting cars, displaying their small, wooden boxes filled with cigarettes, candies and gums to car window after car window. The light turned green, and they ambled back to the sidewalk by the squatter homes where they sat, waiting for the next red light.

The stench grew stronger as we ventured further along the roads next to the hills. On and on it went for miles upon miles. Traffic was terrible, as usual, and I willed in my head to make it move faster. In response, we stopped yet again, at least ten cars down from the light. It was meant to be a four-lane street, but there we were, in the middle of seven cars across. In front of us were eight, behind us, I couldn't tell. No one was moving except for the motocycles weaving in between the cars. I watched enviously as two incredibly large, barefooted men, wearing nothing but undershirts and ripped shorts, passed by us on a tiny scooter. I had no idea how they managed, but that didn't matter. They were ahead. Another one, an entire family of six balancing effortlessly on one motorbike, drove by our jammed hatchback of eight. On the back of the motorbike was a small cage with two chickens inside and two children sitting comfortably on top. How I wished I was one of them.

The smell grew thicker, and it eventually reached a point where it could not get any worse. But by then, my head was dizzy and I covered my nose with both my hands. Even then, the scent seeped between my fingers. I laid my head down on my sister's lap and closed my eyes, hoping to fall back asleep again.

I was awakened by the blast of a car horn, my thoughts as wobbly as my vision. The car was still. I poked my head above my mother's car seat and found no traffic blocking our way, but a pristine, white gate. My father honked again, and the gates opened before us. I only caught a glimpse of the well-manicured trees covering bulky, cake-like pastel mansions in the neighborhood before our car proceeded onto a wide, open driveway. A large, American SUV next to an American sedan rested under the covered ports. The only spot my father could park our tiny, red clown car was a small corner just outside the covered ports. He shut off the engine and proceeded to ogle the SUV. He had always wanted one. *Perfect for the floods,* he would say.

A man my father's age had already greeted my parents warmly by the time the rest of the family had scrambled out of the car.

"Welcome, welcome! Come in, come in!"

They spoke candidly as we were led to heavily ornate double doors.

"Welcome, welcome! Come in, come in!" A strange, overly excited voice echoed.

"Oh my goodness!" my mother exclaimed. "Is that what I think it is?"

Two exotic-looking black birds stood guard within a large, black cage by the entrance. My mother approached them with excitement, gaping at the sight of the two birds rarely seen on our side of the city. She had always been fond of talking birds.

"Oh we have a couple more of those at the back," the man dismissed casually.

We entered the house and stepped onto the cream marbled floor of a sweeping, open hallway with walls reaching high up to the exposed wood beams of the ceiling. A woman—not smiling, nor as excited as the others—welcomed us from the bottom of a wide, dark wooden staircase, which curled in a half circle to a grand balcony on the second floor.

"Welcome..." she said without any expression appearing on her face. "So these are the kids?"

"Yes, this is Annaliza, Aiden, Selina..." my father started pointing to each of us one by one like livestock being presented for auction. "Pauline, Sa-... Sel-... Sephia, and Sabrina," he finished off in his usual name confusion manner.

"Lovely children," she replied.

"Thank you. And kids," said my mother turning to us, "this is Mr. Barahona and Mrs. Barahona. Or you can call them Uncle Josef and Auntie Pearla."

We waved and smiled awkwardly, not a single sound of greeting coming from our lips. She smiled stiffly at each of us, a complete contrast to her husband's calming demeanor.

"Well, Jolina and Jaycee should be coming home from practice soon," said this so-called Uncle Josef. "But we can go ahead and start lunch."

They took us to the adjoining room where a polished, oblong dining table, long enough to sit fourteen, awaited us. The table was already set, complete with heavy china, spoons, forks and knives, paper napkins, a glass and an empty bowl on the side. As we sat down, housekeepers came out with rice and dishes.

"We were going to have a pig roasted, but that may be too much for a small party, so we settled on catering," said Auntie Pearla.

They soon jumped into their grown-up conversations—the politics on which they all agreed on, the gossip about people they knew, the places they'd been to—while my siblings and I sat quietly eating, completely out of our element.

A half hour had passed when we heard the front doors open. A girlish giggle and a long, shrill voice belonging to a little boy filled the hallway. A dark lady walked into the dining room, holding the hands of a little girl—Sonia's age—in a yellow leotard and an even younger boy in a karate uniform.

"I've brought them home, sir," said the lady.

"Good," said Uncle Josef. "Get them ready for lunch."

"Yes, sir."

"Daddy, I want an electric guitar!" the girl cried out of nowhere.

"Me too, Daddy!" the little boy added.

"Yes, yes. Go get changed first," Uncle Josef replied flippantly.

"Electric guitar, Daddy!" the girl insisted before being led out of the room.

Their voices slowly faded as the lady took them away, and we were once again left alone to grown-up conversations and silence. A few minutes later, the two joined us in the dining table. They were never once introduced to us, but I assumed that they were the Jolina and the Jaycee they spoke of earlier. They talked among themselves with Jaycee constantly raising his voice. Now and then, he would shout while slamming his spoon and fork on his plate, followed by a rapid look around the table with a wild, expectant smile. The rest of us could only do our best to ignore him in silence. His sister, on the other hand, would either yell at him to stop or, worse, join him. It was only when it got to at least fifteen seconds of yelling and banging would Uncle Josef or Auntie Pearla interject with a loud PSSSSST, UY! Then the two would return to amusing themselves with their utensils and food while their parents went back to chatting. This routine repeated several times.

Lunch lasted for an uncomfortable hour. My siblings and I left the table the instant we had the chance and huddled together in the sprawling living room, leaving behind the four grown-ups and two loud children. On the opposite end of the room sat a huge, square TV on an expansive shelf where a massive collection of cassette tapes, CDs, video games and various VHS movies were stacked neatly side by side.

"Wow! They have a Nintendo and a VCR!" my brother exclaimed.

My eyes glazed at their collection of movies—specifically the Disney ones—and marveled at the size of a VHS cassette. It looked just like a Betamax except bigger. We gawked and stared, tempted to turn on the TV, but were afraid of what they would say if our fingers smudged anything. We could only gaze longingly from a distance, looking but not touching.

After a while, the novelty of staring at the same expensive looking things wore off, and we wandered off to the sliding door leading to the backyard where the two other talking birds immediately captured our attention. A sprawling spread of grass, neatly trimmed trees and exotic, sharp plants with their spikes covered with bits of square Styrofoam greeted us as we walked toward the large cage big enough to fit both me and Sonia. We stood around it, trying to get the birds to talk with a convoluted chorus of "hellos" and repetitions of our names. The birds only stared at us in mild curiosity.

"*Hoy!*" we heard a boy's cry. "What are you doing?! Those are our birds!"

Jaycee was right next to us within seconds, pushing and shoving us away from the cage.

"You can't play with them! You didn't ask first! Our birds! Not yours!"

"Jaycee! Let them play with the birds!" his father yelled from the sliding door. We turned to see my parents, Uncle Josef and Auntie Pearla milling about the same living room we vacated earlier. "Go on kids. Don't worry about him," he said, turning to us.

We returned back to the birds, but by then, we were all feeling too shy and uncomfortable, even with each other, with a moody, pouting boy standing in front of us.

"Jaycee, come here!" his sister called out, running next to him. In her hand was a Barbie doll. Its clean outfit and face indicated that it was new, but its wild, stringy hair said otherwise. She stopped by her brother's side with a wide grin, her eyes darting from face to face before finally resting on Sonia's.

"Hey, come play tag with us!"

My sister didn't say a word.

"Come on, play!" she demanded, stomping a foot.

Sonia stared at her for a few seconds, then looked down to the ground before looking up and turning quickly away toward the house, straight to my mother's side.

"What's the matter?" my mother asked as Sonia crept close to her leg. "You should be outside." She took her hand and led her out to the bird cage.

"Play with us!" Jolina cried as they approached. "Come on, play!"

"Go on, play with them," my mother urged my sister. Sonia looked imploringly at each of us, her eyes pleading for a way out. We all ignored her, afraid to defy my ever commanding, forceful mother. Still, Sonia did not move. My mother gave an annoyed sighed.

"Pauline, go join your sister!" she barked at me. My eyes grew wide in bewilderment, my mouth moving open, about sputter out an objection, but one look at my mother's lightning stare...

"Ok..." I said, meekly.

Sonia and I walked, resigned in our matching blue, plaid dresses, following the trail of the two children running off. I glanced back to see my mother joining my older siblings around the cage. The look on my older sisters' faces spoke of relief at finally being left alone, in spite of their two youngest sisters being picked out like sacrificial lambs to these two overly excited children.

"So..." said Jolina eagerly as she spun around. "Who's going to be 'it' first?"

"One of them! One of them!" Jaycee pointed at us, hopping up and down.

"No, you!" said his sister. "You're the only boy, so you're 'it.'"

"What?! No way!" But Jolina had already run off.

Sonia and I glanced at each other quickly then took off in the same direction. I heard some angry shrieking and stomping behind me, but I kept my pace, not running too fast because, after all, what were the chances that some younger kid could catch up to me?

A very high chance, apparently, especially if that younger kid happened to be that particular boy. I did not look behind me, but I knew that excited shriek and hard fist punching the back of my head could have only come from that crazed child. The blow knocked me off balance, and I stumbled onto the ground, my stiff, plaid dress flipping up on my legs and exposing my underwear.

"*TAYA*! You're 'it'!" Jaycee screeched. I looked up from the ground to see him run off, not exactly away from me as I expected, but more toward my sister. His hand bundled into a fist and swung into the air. It was a sloppy swing, but the force and intent were there. It collided with Sonia's cheek as she turned her face and, like me, was knocked to the ground with a look of disbelief on her face.

"You too! You're *taya*!" he giggled as he ran off. *That's not how you play the game*, I thought to myself. But no matter. I got up and walked to where Sonia, still slightly disoriented from the hit, was kneeling on the ground.

"That hurt," I said sheepishly, rubbing the back of my head.

"Hey! Who's 'it'?" Jolina had rushed back to our side. Sonia and I looked at each. We didn't quite know how to answer her exactly.

"I don't know..." I started when suddenly my head snapped backward, stinging from my hair being pulled.

"It's her! I got her first!" Jaycee was right behind me, yanking my hair.

"Stop it!" I yelled, but he only pulled harder, gleefully laughing. I grabbed his arm and pulled my head back. He let go, but slapped me on my ear—likely from missing my face.

"And then she's 'it' next!" he pointed to my sister. "I got her after!"

"What...?" My sister and I looked at each other, thoroughly confused.

"That's not how you play that game, Jaycee," said Jolina in an annoyed voice. "You can't tag two people at once."

"But that's how I want to play it!"

"But it's my rules, and my rules say no double-tagging."

"Ugh, fine! Let's play monsters then!"

"Monsters?" I asked.

"Yes! I'll be the monster and you guys have to stop me!" And with that, he began making roaring noises, moving toward us.

Jolina began to squeal and run around him.

"We have to stop him!" she cried. "We must destroy the monster!"

Sonia and I, not knowing exactly what to do, began to run around as well. He had already kicked my sister to the ground and was on his way toward me when I began to run faster, not wanting this "monster" to catch up to me.

"No, no! You have to stop him! Face him!" I heard Jolina cry out. *As if I wanted to do that*.

"RAAAWWRRR!" he growled as ferociously as a five year old could muster. He ran over and picked up a small wooden chair nearby and started chasing us. He swung the chair at me, one of its stumpy legs scraping my arm. Another swing and it struck my elbow. *That's gonna bruise*, I thought to myself.

"Stop him, stop him!" Jolina kept crying out. "He's coming this way!" Never once did he go after her, I noticed, as he threw the chair at Sonia, missing her. It was always either me or Sonia.

"I am the great *halimaw*!" he shouted, picking up the tossed chair and holding it over his head. "I will kill all of you!" He began to move closer, slowly stomping his feet one by one like the giant beast he was supposed to be. "Kill! Kill! Kill!" His face contorted into a bizarre snarl and, with one final roar, came forward with the chair above his head, not seeing a short, empty plant pot in front of him. In one swift motion, he lost his footing on the pot and lightly fell forward onto the grass, dropping the chair in front of him. To the three of us standing a few feet away from him, it was an innocent fall—nothing painful, nothing hilarious. Just a simple fall that any child could easily get up from. But no, not to him. Not to Jaycee.

He stayed on the ground, utterly confused at first. But then he turned bright red and began to cry. It wasn't just any ordinary cry. Not a cry from someone who had simply tripped over a pot. No, it was the cry of someone who had fallen off a cliff and broken every single bone in their body. He screeched and cried, then pointed his finger angrily at my sister and me.

"YOU!" he shrieked. "It was you two! It's all your fault!"

"What?" I asked, incredulously. "How?"

"Both of you made me fall!"

"But we were just standing here..."

"No, you made me fall! I fell because of you two!"

I turned to Jolina, hoping she could say something, anything, to make him see sense, perhaps even slap him around in the same manner he tried to slap us around. But instead, I found a face that, although calm, was just as accusing as her younger brother's. She looked at us, stringy Barbie still gripped in her hands.

"It's your fault..." she whispered.

"Both your fault!" Jaycee added.

"*Lagot kayo*," she said. "You're both in big trouble."

"We didn't do anything!" I repeated.

"I'm telling mommy!" Jaycee cried.

"Yes, we're gonna tell our mommy!" And with that, the two deranged children ran toward the house.

"Wait! We didn't do anything!" I called after them, but they didn't seem to hear nor care. I wanted to stop them like a guilty child who was about to be exposed, though in my head I knew that Sonia and I didn't do anything wrong. But knowing my parents' temperamental ways, it never really mattered whose fault it was. If any one of us cried over anything, that meant lying face down on the bed and feeling the lash of the belt on our bottoms and thighs.

They were telling on us. *That's not fair*, I thought. *He hit us first.* The fearful feeling in my chest sunk into the pit of my stomach, completely replaced by a simmering anger. It filled my lungs, taking root and rising up to my reddening face and stinging eyes. I ran to my mother who was still standing with my siblings around the bird cage. I blabbered to her everything that happened, from the punching to the falling.

"*Aynaku*," was all she said. "Come, stay next to me." She did not walk over to those two kids to yell at them as she would've done had it been us. She simply took our hands and walked us both over to the living room. In there, Jaycee was still crying on his mother's lap, while Jolina stood next to her father.

116

"It was their fault! They made me fall!" Jaycee pointed to us just as we walked in.

"We didn't do anything," I whispered softly. "He fell on his own." I wanted to add more, tell them how he hit us, pulled our hairs and kicked us. But from the look on his mother's face, I somehow knew it was pointless. She stared at me and my sister for a long while with expressionless eyes, then turned away.

"Beth, take the kids upstairs," she said to one of the housekeepers. The same dark lady we saw earlier came and took Jolina and Jaycee by the hands and led them upstairs. Nothing else was said. No scolding, no punishment. I knew from the look in her flat eyes that she either did not believe us or considered whatever Jaycee did to be completely acceptable, but we still shouldn't have made him cry.

"Why don't you and your sister go join the others outside?" said my mother.

We didn't say anything but just walked away, defeated and embarrassed. We joined my other siblings outside, still around the bird cage, all of them pretending as if nothing had happened. The sun had already begun to peek out from the gloomy skies. Although still feeling angry and ashamed, at least I was relieved at no longer being forced to play with those two. I wanted so badly for my parents to finish up whatever it was they came here for, go home and be left alone. I didn't really care how big their house was or anything about the talking birds. I wanted out.

But after a few minutes of sitting around my siblings, my tightened fists began to slacken and my head cooled a little. Even my siblings seemed to relax. They joked and chatted, appearing more comfortable than earlier. I felt my stiff limbs slacking. Finally, I was calm again.

But of course, that didn't last too long. Because within minutes, Jaycee and Jolina were back, running around the backyard. From the way they were laughing and scampering about, it was obvious that they too had gotten over the accident that Sonia and I supposedly caused earlier. Tension clenched its way back into my fists as they inched closer, but I ignored them, even as they laughed louder, their eyes flying back and forth between me and my sister. They were playing that monster game again, I noticed.

"RAWR! The *halimaw* has returned!" Jaycee yelled. Although it was directed at his sister, his eyes were turned toward me. I looked away, not caring about this *halimaw*. He roared and ran around in front of us, but we took no notice of him. He stood up and jumped off the short concrete wall where I sat and even picked up the same wooden chair he threw around earlier. Yet we continued to ignore him. At some point, he finally gave up and just included us nevertheless, whether we wanted to or not. He snuck up behind me and Sonia as we stood by the bird cage and grabbed a fistful of hair.

"I got you now!"

I held back on my urge to swing my fists behind me, knowing that if this crazy boy would wail over a minor fall of his own doing and have his parents believe that it was our fault, I could only imagine what he would be like if I actually punched him on purpose.

"Let go of my head," I said through gritted teeth, my hands tightly clamping the metal lines of the cage. He yanked our heads backs before running off. My sister looked at me with fire in her eyes, the same angry spark that I was sure was flashing in my own.

I supposed that we were meant to chase after him, but there was just nothing in this whole wide world that could make me join him and his sister again. They began to realize this as my sister and I continued to ignore them. Soon they were next to us, openly and unabashedly begging us to play with them.

"Why don't you play with us?"

"C'mon, join us!"

No, that's ok. No, we don't want to, my sister and I recited repetitiously like the litany of Our Fathers and the Hail Marys of the rosary, wishing for our prayers to be answered and finally be left alone. But no.

"For crying out loud, just go play with them!" my mother finally yelled to us. We could only look at her helplessly before we resigned ourselves to what we figured would be another round of punches and kicks. Fortunately, the two had already expended their energy and were too tired for another round of violent tag. Instead, they wanted to show us their rooms.

We climbed up the wide arching stairway to the brightened balcony with wall-to-wall sliding windows that lead to an outdoor balcony. The open space steered into a darkened hallway to the left where we followed the two to one of the doorways. My eyes adjusted as Jolina opened a door to a sunny room.

"This is my room," said a proud Jolina.

It was an enormous bedroom, at least by my standards. Daylight beamed from the broad bay windows and the slanted skylight above a full-sized bed. The hardwood floors gleamed as if freshly waxed, adding shine to the already bright room. Although the room itself was impressive to behold, my eyes were drawn to the multiple layers of shelves on the walls.

Rows upon rows of Barbie dolls—still packaged neatly in their boxes—were arranged like ornamental porcelain. I gaped with wonder. Never mind that they were still in boxes, these were the toys I'd always wanted to play with. Not that my American cousin's old toys were anything to complain about, of course. I still liked the stuffed dolls and action figures that they sent over to us from the States, but they certainly did not come in these numbers.

"My room next!" Jaycee announced.

We walked to an adjoining bedroom connected to Jolina's through a doorway next to her private bathroom. Jaycee's room was just as impressive in size and in its collection of toys. Instead of boxed Barbies and others dolls, the shelves on the walls were lined with action figures and dinosaurs still in their packaging. I could see how proud they were. I knew I would be too if I were in their shoes.

"Let's go watch a movie!" They walked us to the opposite end of the hallway to the other side of the balcony where a lonely doorway led to another large room with high ceilings. There was exercise equipment, weights and a treadmill. There was also a couch, a beanbag and another huge square TV. We sat down while they had a different housekeeper put in Sleeping Beauty on the VCR. We watched for the rest of the afternoon until my parents finally called us downstairs.

"Time to go!" they called to us.

Sonia and I dragged ourselves downstairs while Jaycee and Jolina remained glued to the carpet in front of the TV. We were both exhausted from the afternoon.

My parents said their farewells and, as we packed ourselves back into the little red coup and pulled out of their driveway—away from the huge house full of toys and video games, movies and talking birds—I couldn't help but feel a strange tug in my chest, a mixture of relief and envy. I wanted to stay there in that big house and play with all their toys, but at the same time, I didn't want to be there with those two. An hour of going through their inventory of toys and then watching a cartoon in peace wasn't enough to assuage my memory of that sadistic game of tag.

We drove away from the quiet neighborhood of big cake houses and tall trees, slowly easing our way back into our loud, bustling side of the city. The colorful yellow and pink houses began to disappear, replaced by grey buildings and charcoal roads. Exhaustion wrapped itself around me, and I fell asleep on my sister's lap again. The afternoon sunlight radiated onto my face, and beads of sweat formed around my neck and back. The noxious scent from earlier began to crawl its way back to my nostrils. I woke up with a grimace only to see the long, desolate road through the Smokey Mountains. The scent of the landfill, baking under the afternoon sun and fusing with the humidity, was far more potent than before. I couldn't go back to sleep after that and had to endure the remainder of the long drive home.

"Did you guys have fun?" my father asked from the driver's seat.

"Sure," we responded robotically.

"They're very nice people," said my mother.

"Yes, very nice people," my father replied.

"I don't know about their kids though. They seemed to have trouble with our girls. Do you think they'll invite us again?" my mother asked.

"I don't know. They might."

The scowling look Auntie Pearla gave us as we repacked ourselves into the car and just before we drove off told me otherwise. And sure enough, we were never invited again.

Tropic of Ennui
by Subashini Navaratnam

All my life, I've been preparing
to take KL with me, to run with
my home on my back, as though
the present has already congealed
at the bottom of the rice pot, a sticky
brown residue that scrubbing doesn't
remove. I've lived through the enervating
heat of a thousand blooming Julys,
waved my clothesline like a flag for peace.
Perspiration is my known foe.

Smell the smog in the brief coolness
of the tropical morning as it hesitates
before unleashing the slow fire of the day.
Watch a smug face from inside
an air-conditioned BMW speed up
next to the weary face on the back
of a motorbike, carrying a stick of bamboo,
battling the elements on every ride along
highways that snake across where
the former wetlands used to be.

Citizens of the republic of mud,

we have started to taste the smoke and see

the sea gone red. Home is where the heart

has been made to censor itself so that

life can proceed like the arrival of dusk.

Everyone with their head down, dreams

tucked into their sleeves and prowling locked

rooms, willing themselves to stay tame

so that they might live another day to sell

what their body can do.

You had an understanding about the future:

It would be bright like a green age and it would be desired.

Now it rests on pavements like black crows

shot by DBKL: inky petals on grey concrete,

feathers still in the motionless air.

Didith's Boyfriend
by Raymund P. Reyes

It was the woman's uncanny resemblance to his late wife that caught his attention—the short, stick-thin figure with disproportionately rounded hips, walking in three-inch heels in the fast, shuffling steps of one who seemed to be in a constant hurry. A bob cut dyed chestnut brown framed a face with an expression of intense concentration. On top of that, the woman was wearing a white blouse with large *gumamela* prints and ruffles around the shoulders, the very same one his wife had in her closet.

Ramon was riding his motorcycle on his way to work in Manila when he saw her. The woman was walking on the sidewalk with other passengers who were left stranded after the *jeepney* they were riding broke down in the middle of the road. It was seven in the morning, and the sun already burned. It was also the rush hour, and Ramon knew that most *jeepneys* passing by would be full and, unless these passengers walked to a *jeepney* terminal in a supermarket five blocks away, it would be impossible for them to get another ride. He skidded to a halt beside her, and pushed the visor of his helmet up to speak to her.

"Hi! You must be one of the passengers from the *jeepney* that stalled back there. Umm ... you might not take to strangers but ... I saw you and I told myself, with those shoes, she might be suffering. Would you consider an offer of a ride?"

The woman was taken aback at Ramon's offer.

"Did I scare you? Oh, sorry. I'm Ramon." He extended his hand. The woman took it hesitantly.

"No, I'll be fine. But thank you. Another *jeepney* is bound to pass by soon."

"I don't think so, ma'am. This is rush hour, so unless you walk the five blocks to the supermarket ... in your heels and with this heat..."

"But I don't think you have an extra helmet for me." She looked over his red Honda motorcycle.

"You can borrow mine. I don't mind. And it's just to the marketplace. It's a short ride on my motorbike, but a long walk for you. If you want to get to your office on time ... and considering what you're wearing..." He glanced down at her feet.

The woman paused and stared at Ramon, as if trying to weigh the sincerity of his offer. She looked around at her fellow passengers. Some waited by the sidewalk while others, like her, had begun the trek to the supermarket.

"Okay, I'll take it," she nodded her head in assent. He offered to help her mount behind him, but to his surprise, she easily positioned herself sitting sideways and placed one heeled shoe on the foot peg.

"I used to ride with my brother when I was younger," she said. "This was like decades ago." She smiled self-consciously.

Ramon then took off his helmet and gave it to her. She refused with a wave of her hand and told him she'd be fine. She grabbed on to the rail around the seat and, in spite his suggestion, resisted the urge to grab on to his waist.

"What's your name?" Ramon asked his passenger.

The ride took about five minutes, but that first question was enough to start a conversation. Over the roar of the engine, he learned that her name was Didith, that she was a professor of Philippine history in a Catholic college in Manila, she was a spinster who lived with an older sister who was also an old maid in a house left to them by their late parents, and that her favorite food was sweet *hopia*, a flaky pastry with mung bean filling. When he dropped her off by the *jeepney* terminal in the supermarket, he was also able to get her mobile phone number.

Ramon courted Didith the old-fashioned way. He would visit every Saturday afternoon from two to six—came and left on the dot each time. He always brought with him a box of a particular brand of her favorite *hopia*, which he had to buy in the Chinatown district of Binondo because Didith did not like the kind which could be bought in every other bakery. He would not stay beyond 6pm because Didith would then be having dinner with her siblings, who openly despised his intrusion into their sister's life.

The eldest, Lorraine, never let her younger sister out of her sight whenever Ramon visited. If the two decided to talk under the mango tree in the yard, Lorraine would be looking out the window from her bedroom upstairs, knitting while stealing glances at them. If they decided to stay in the living room, Lorraine would be by the rocking chair in the foyer, still knitting but obviously eavesdropping on the conversation. And on her face she kept a sour expression—brows furrowed and thin lips pursed tightly.

Didith wasn't exactly a maiden who needed to be kept under close watch. In fact at forty years old, she was already what would be labeled as an "old maid". Lorraine's over-protectiveness of her younger sister was borne out of a personal bitterness and distrust against men. Lorraine, who would turn fifty in a couple of months, almost got married when she was thirty before her groom-to-be decided to elope with an old girlfriend who came home from abroad, supposedly to attend the wedding. From then on, Lorraine swore off men and thought Didith would do well to be rid of them, too. Of course, when Didith had asked her what she found offensive about Ramon, Lorraine told her that it was because Ramon was a lowly clerk in city hall. She thought that someone with a Ph.D. like Didith deserved someone better.

The second sibling, Dodong, lived next door but mostly spent his weekends in the ancestral home—especially for meals—because he could not stand his maid's cooking. Meanwhile, Didith had always been the cook in the family, a skill she gained from summers during her childhood that she spent in culinary schools. Dodong had been married before, but when his only daughter turned eighteen and decided to continue studying in America, his wife went with their daughter, and he had never heard from the wife since. The daughter hadn't come home for the last four years, although she called during special days like Christmas and her father's birthday. It was she who relayed to him the news that her mother had no more plans of ever coming back to the Philippines. She had found someone else—a butcher—and moved in with him two weeks after they met.

If Lorraine's issue with Ramon was the fact that he was a man, Dodong's opposition stemmed from the belief that the man was only after Didith's money. While only earning the salary of a college professor, Didith and her two siblings were left a sizeable trust fund by their late parents. They also received regular income from the rice fields in Batangas, which were also part of their inheritance. Dodong was a chief accountant in a bank in Quezon City while Lorraine had chosen not to work and simply managed their farmlands as well as the lives of her brother and sister.

Ever since Ramon began his regular visits, Dodong stopped coming to the house for free meals on Saturdays, and he did not keep the reason for his staying away a secret. The first time that Ramon showed himself on the doorstep, Dodong only gave him a nod and nothing more.

As soon as the antique grandfather clock by the foyer struck six, Ramon would bid his goodbyes. Lorraine would stop her knitting and walk in the direction of the dining room. Then, once the roar of Ramon's motorcycle was out of earshot, she would ask for half of the box of *hopia* from her sister. It was also a favorite of hers.

Didith had suitors when she was younger, but her siblings found fault with every one of them and would vocalize their criticisms against these men: not good-looking enough, too effeminate to be straight, not smart enough for a bright girl, easy-go-lucky and irresponsible, etc. On her part, Didith had always relied on her siblings' opinions. She loved them that much. She was a baby when both parents died in a plane crash. Lorraine had been like a mother to her, and so she valued her approval to whatever decision she had to make.

However, Didith liked Ramon from that very first day from the side of the road. She would constantly replay in her mind the moment he opened the visor of his helmet, smiled at her and offered her a ride. She couldn't pinpoint exactly why she liked him at that time or what had attracted him to her. He wasn't good-looking in her opinion, though the dimple on his right cheek certainly helped. She also noticed how his eyes wrinkled at the edges when he smiled. The fact that he showed sympathy for her poor feet while walking in heels that morning and singled her out from the other passengers was also a plus. He was obviously much younger than her—more than a decade younger—and for a younger man to notice someone her age was a compliment in itself. He had not told her, however, about her resemblance to his late wife nor showed her a picture, although Ramon had told her about being a widower after his wife died from cancer three years earlier.

If Ramon had not insisted on courting her properly, she knew that she would have confessed her affection for him on that very first afternoon when he showed up on the doorstep carrying a box of her favorite sweet *hopia*. A day after their chance encounter, he had phoned her. And every night afterward, he would call to say goodnight. After a week, he mustered the courage to ask her whether he could stop by her house for a visit as he could not stop thinking about her. Didith was immediately smitten, and it took the utmost effort to maintain her image as a conservative and traditional Filipina. It had been a long time since someone had shown interest in her. When she reached thirty, the men seemed to have stricken her off from their list of prospects. Those who didn't know her assumed she was already married. Many times when she lay in bed at night, she would regret the lost years.

Didith had been honest to Ramon about her siblings' opinion of him and asked for his understanding. He only loved her more knowing that she continued to give him a chance in spite of the fact that Lorraine— whom he knew Didith loved more than any person in the world—was against him. He promised her that in deference to her sister and brother, he would not propose marriage until she had convinced them that he only had noble intentions for her. Even if it took him years to persuade them, he said. He wasn't in a hurry. Only her love for him mattered.

Ramon and Didith soon developed a routine aside from the Saturday visits. Every morning, Ramon would fetch Didith from the house. He had brought her a helmet so she could ride with him. He even remembered to get an orange helmet as it was her favorite color. He dropped her off at the college where she taught. Then in the afternoon, he would pick her up so they could ride home together. On Saturdays he would visit in the afternoon, always bringing with him a box of sweet *hopia*. Some weekends, though, they would go out of town on his motorcycle to Tagaytay, Laguna, Antipolo or Bulacan. Dodong had stopped worrying once he learned that Ramon didn't intend to marry his sister. Lorraine could only watch with indignation from her upstairs window as Ramon and Didith drove off for their weekend date.

The siblings were invited by a cousin in London to attend a wedding. In the last week of November, the three flew for London. Their plan was to travel around Europe for three weeks before the wedding, which was set on the twentieth of December. They were to fly back to Manila on Christmas day. But health concerns unexpectedly shortened their trip.

Didith first complained of a headache on the flight to Europe. She slept through most of the flight, waking up only once for a four-hour stopover in Dubai. She appeared lively, window-shopping in the duty-free shops of the huge airport. She was in the same upbeat mood when they arrived at Heathrow. She mentioned the pain intermittently for the next few days but would dismiss them as simply being a series of migraine attacks, a condition which she had been suffering from and taking medication for years now. But a week later, while they were in the train terminal bound for Paris, she lost consciousness in the departure lounge. They brought her to the nearest hospital, where she came to a couple of hours later. A scan revealed a malignant tumor in her brain. They were all surprised because she didn't show any symptoms before aside from the recent headaches. Didith confessed to having experienced several painful episodes for a year now, but she assumed it was only her migraine getting worse.

The specialist who diagnosed Didith recommended immediate surgery to remove the tumor before it caused an aneurysm which, in turn, could lead to death. The siblings immediately rebooked their tickets and got on the earliest flight back to Manila. They couldn't have the surgery done in London because it would be too expensive. As it were, Didith's credit card was almost maxed out from the hospital bills they had incurred from her brief hospitalization.

However, events happened faster than expected. Right after the plane landed in Manila, Didith suffered a stroke. She was brought by airport paramedics to the hospital. The stroke rendered the left side of her body paralyzed. The surgeon then told her that the tumor was of considerable size and that taking it out at that point posed the risk of affecting her mental faculties, thereby worsening her already deplorable condition. Her speech slurred and stuttering, Didith told her brother and sister that she would rather die on her own terms than live longer but lose the ability of being aware of the things going on around her. She requested them to call Ramon and let him know about her condition. In the flurry of events, no one had remembered to inform him about Didith's condition.

Ramon left work and went directly to the hospital after receiving Lorraine's call. When he arrived, Lorraine was on a visitor's couch adjacent to the bed, knitting a shawl. She had brought a maid along, seated on a chair beside the patient's bed watching a game show on a television mounted high on the opposite wall. Without a word, Lorraine simply pointed at her sister and motioned for the maid to accompany her outside. This time, she had a stoic expression on her face, an improvement from the disapproving glare she always had ready for Didith's boyfriend before.

Ramon stayed the whole night and only went out to have dinner in the hospital cafeteria. Lorraine went home with the maid after visiting hours ended.

Didith died at three in the morning with Ramon by her bedside.

The wake lasted for five nights, and Ramon was there each night. He went home from work to have dinner and change clothes before proceeding to the funeral parlor. He sat by himself on the front pew and didn't talk to anyone, simply staring into space. Sometimes his eyes would close, as if asleep or in prayer. They were bloodshot, but no one saw him cry. The relatives and the other visitors there knew of Didith and Ramon's story, but they kept their distance. No one dared to talk to him, afraid that Dodong and Lorraine might be offended if they approached the boyfriend whom the family disapproved of. He would leave at midnight, walking out of the room as quietly as he had come.

On the fourth night, Lorraine noticed tears streaming down Ramon's face. He must have been unconscious about them falling since he didn't wipe them away. He kept his head up like a statue, watching a point in space. She finally took pity on him—sitting alone in front of the room just a few meters away from Didith's coffin—while the rest of the guests chatted in the back pews. Lorraine sat beside him. She took his hand into her own without saying a word. Ramon gasped and breathed heavily to control his sobs. The two sat without saying a word to each other, but Lorraine knew at that moment that whatever ill feelings she had for him had gone.

Ramon didn't show up for Didith's funeral the following day.

Two months had passed since the funeral. Lorraine visited her sister's grave in the cemetery. It was a Friday afternoon just before sunset. It had become her habit to visit every Saturday, but she was going to attend a conference in Baguio and would be leaving very early in the morning so she decided to go a day earlier.

She saw Ramon's now familiar red Honda motorcycle in the parking lot by the gate of the cemetery. She caught the man sitting cross-legged on the grass before the headstone, a marble slab with an angel statue standing over it. She knew Ramon also regularly visited Didith's grave because every time she came on Saturdays, there would always be a fresh bouquet of roses on the gravestone. She knew only Ramon would go to the trouble. His elder brother had been promoted to regional manager and assigned to Cebu a week after Didith's death. In fact, she had not seen or talked to Dodong even once since he left.

Surprised, Ramon stood up when he saw Lorraine approach. She offered her hand in greeting. Conversation began awkwardly, but they were soon candidly sharing happy memories they had had with Didith. Only the happy memories. So engrossed in their conversation, they didn't even notice that the sun had set and that the air had turned chilly until Lorraine felt the annoying itch of a mosquito bite and realized how late it had become. Ramon asked Lorraine whether he could give her a lift home on his motorcycle. She refused, apologizing for not being as daring as her late sister when it came to riding motorcycles.

It wasn't the last time that the two chanced upon each other at Didith's grave. It seemed as if an unspoken agreement had been shared between them from that first meeting. She learned that Ramon went to the cemetery every Friday directly after work. From then on, Lorraine would also visit the cemetery on Friday afternoons to keep Ramon company and to talk with someone who loved her sister as much as she did.

One Saturday afternoon, Lorraine was in her bedroom upstairs knitting a shawl when the doorbell rang. She looked out the window and saw Ramon by the gate dismounting from his motorcycle. It had been a year since he last set foot in the house. Lorraine nonetheless went down and let him in. In his hands, Ramon carried a box of sweet *hopia*, which he handed to her upon stepping into the foyer.

The Fish Ponds of Laos
by Reed Venrick

On top of Vang Vieng's morning hills, trying to see through
the foggy nightmare of history's pock-marked valley

and searching further east over blazing fields, I
peer into, while holding up the broken fragments

of, the Plain of Jars, where the great hawks flew
with demonic power and defecated an ocean of bombs

for another generation to swim and pass to memory—
I ride the old motorbike again to the summit

and feel the shock of monsoon lightning that broke
the jars that spilled the water oozing from the Mekong.

Ah, but history designs its irony in the perfection
of circles that mark the horizon's rice fields,

and if one peers far enough, the out-of-school children
jumping and diving and splashing

and at dusk, the old farmer comes to shoo them away,
hanging out the bamboo pole, wetting a fishing line

in the fountain of the Mekong watershed

for minnows to begin again to swim round

the vicious circle of targeted blueprints

turned to ponds of water where generations

reincarnate and priests speak quietly of peace

and moon-perfect nights when the great jars

will be glued together again and hold the ancient water.

Me and Kap Chai
by Chang Shih Yen

I think it was *The Motorcycle Diaries* that first put the idea in my head. In the movie, which was based on real events, Che Guevara rides a motorcycle across South America with his friend, Alberto Granado. They rode from Buenos Aires, the capital of Argentina, to Chile and then north to Peru. They rode practically the whole length of South America on a 1939 Norton 500cc motorcycle. The movie planted a small seed that slowly grew in my mind, and when the conditions were right, it burst forth like a little shoot unfurling its first green leaf.

My opportunity came when things started going a bit shitty in my life. First, I lost my job. Then my girlfriend dumped me. Neither was a big surprise. The company I worked for had been "restructuring" for months, and my girlfriend and I had been fighting. I was one of the many foreigners who lived in Singapore solely to earn a living. So after all of that happened, I found myself with no reason to be in Singapore anymore.

I moped around in my room for a few weeks wondering what to do with my life. My future seemed to be a big, black gaping hole. Logic and reason told me that I needed to get my act together, write a resume and start applying for another job, but my body wasn't listening to reason. That was when that little idea, which had been burning on a low flame somewhere in the back of my mind, came to the fore again.

If Che could ride his unreliable motorcycle across South America, back in the days before computers and cell phones, why couldn't I do the same through South East Asia in this modern day and age? *What was stopping me*? *Nothing*! I didn't have a job, or a girlfriend or any children to tie me down. What was I doing with my free time anyway? I hadn't been looking for a new job. All I was doing was playing computer games all day. And I actually did own a motorcycle. I looked at maps online to plan out a route. Yeah, I knew that I could totally do this.

So I got rid of almost all of my stuff. I didn't have much to begin with anyway as I was only renting a room in Singapore. Possessions can be like shackles that tie you down, and as the number of things I owned decreased, my sense of freedom steadily increased. The biggest thing I owned was my motorbike. It wasn't anything fancy—a blue Honda EX5 Dream—a very common bike all across South East Asia. Che named his motorbike La Poderosa ("the powerful"), despite its many breakdowns. I supposed that for such a long journey, I should give my ride a name too, much like naming a horse.

People tend to look down on my type of lightweight motorbike and disparagingly call them *kap chai* ("little cub"). Still, my bike had been modified, so it went a bit faster than the regular Hondas, and I could take it on the highway. I figured that Kap Chai was as good a name as any. So I readied myself for an uninhibited, single life on the road.

I gave notice on my rented room, tied a small bag onto the back of my motorbike and that was it. I was ready to leave. The remainder of my worldly possessions was on the back of that bike. There was no fixed plan other than to use up all my savings and see how far I could get on my motorbike. Only when I ran out of money would I worry about looking for a job again.

And just like that, I was on my way. For the first time in months, I felt free. No work, no stress, no girlfriend problems, no timetables, no meetings, no appointments to keep. It was just me and the open road.

At first, it felt strange to be going solo. I usually had my girlfriend riding pillion behind me with her hands around my waist. But that feeling didn't last long. In the excitement of starting this trip, I realized that I didn't miss her at all. I headed north, passed the Woodlands Check Point and found myself on the Causeway leaving Singapore and starting my adventure. The further away from Singapore I got, the more I felt my problems and worries melt away. It wasn't long before I was in Johor, the southernmost state of West Malaysia. I had left behind the cleanliness and ordered skyscrapers of Singapore for the gritty chaos of Johor Bahru.

Once in Johor, I wondered what to do. There was a Legoland, a Hello Kitty Town and a Thomas Town, but that was the domain of children and families—not something I was interested in. I was starving, though, so I went in search of a good duck restaurant that I had heard was located very near to the Singapore-Johor border.

I spotted the restaurant in a row of old, dilapidated shop lots. Neatly arranged roast ducks hung on hooks at the front of the restaurant welcoming me. I went in and ordered their specialty: herbal roast duck. When my meal arrived, the duck meat was almost swimming in their famous herbal sauce, and the duck skin glistened with a bronze hue under the fluorescent lights. I ate it all up, soaking up the sauce with white rice.

After lunch, I decided that I needed dessert. There was a well-known bakery very nearby. It had been around for almost a century, and it still baked its goods in an old-fashioned, wood-fired oven. The bakery's fresh cakes and buns are so popular that a long queue would form every morning and stretch all the way outside. I bought a light, moist and fragrant banana cake, their signature product. Well-fed and happy, it was time to hit the road again. I took the highway northwest up the Malay Peninsula.

Travelling on a motorbike is different from being inside a car. On a bike, you feel everything more intensely: every pothole, every bump in the road. You smell all the smells: the exhaust fumes, the trash in open drains, the smell of fried foods from roadside stalls. There is no air conditioning, and you are completely exposed to the whims of the weather. A motorbike removes the barrier between driver and the surroundings.

The long, gray highway stretched out in front of me while the blue sky sat above. I loved it when the highway passed through jungles, and I was surrounded by lush greenery. There was something peaceful about that, and it made me feel closer to nature.

It was a long ride before I reached Malacca. When I got to the city, I was ready for a rest. Being seated in the same position for hours left muscles I didn't even know I had feeling achy, as if I had been working out at the gym.

I found a budget hotel for the night. It didn't have air conditioning, but it was cheap and had a bed without any bed bugs to rest my weary body. I awoke the next morning to find that none of my possessions had been stolen overnight. That's all I could have asked for from a budget hotel.

I checked out of the hotel early and resumed my journey. I rode around Malacca city in what turned out to be a fun drive. Getting out so early allowed me to see many of the historical attractions while beating the normal traffic congestion and overbearing heat.

There was so much history crammed within a small area of the city. I started on St. Paul's Hill, where I saw the sixteenth-century ruins of the Portuguese-built St. Paul's Church. At the bottom of the hill were the remnants of the Portuguese A Famosa fort. Nearby along the banks of the Malacca River was the Maritime Museum, housed in a life-size replica of a sixteenth-century Portuguese ship named *Flor do Mar* ("Flower of the Sea").

Around the corner was the section of the city that the Dutch built in the seventeenth century. The distinctively deep red color of the Stadthuys, its matching clock tower and the adjacent Christ Church are iconic. By comparison, the nineteenth-century Catholic Church of St. Francis Xavier seemed new next to all the other buildings I had seen.

I then went to see Hang Li Poh's well, which was built for one of the wives of fifteenth-century Malaccan Sultan Mansur Syah. The well was not much to look at; it was just a hole in the ground. What made it special was that it had been built in 1459, making it the oldest known well in Malaysia. There was so much more to see in Malacca, and I was reluctant to leave.

I took one last spin around the city while looking at the old Peranakan buildings before riding into the small state of Negeri Sembilan. In its capital, Seremban, I stopped at the main market in the middle of town, to eat its famous Seremban beef noodles. I ordered the dry beef noodles in a dark sauce as this type is unique to Seremban. My beef noodles arrived with fat, white rice noodles that looked a bit like Japanese udon noodles. The noodles were topped with prime cuts of beef, pickled cabbage, peanuts, a generous sprinkling of sesame seeds and the famous thick, brown sauce. I stirred everything together until the contents of my bowl looked like a gooey brown mess, and then ate it all up. The combination of flavors danced a very satisfying tango on my tongue, while the cacophony of noises and voices in the market's food court washed over me.

After lunch I rode the relatively short distance to Kuala Lumpur, the Malaysian capital. KL was the worst part of my journey, though partly because it rained heavily just as I arrived. It was the type of torrential monsoon rain that came down like a blinding wall of water. I could hardly see in front of me. And I didn't have a rain coat or anything to keep me dry, so I resorted to finding shelter under a flyover with other motorcyclists until the worst of the rain was over.

Another problem was the traffic, the gridlocked roads resembling a jumbled mess of spaghetti dropped onto the map. Inevitably I got lost even with the help of GPS. I gave up after trying to make sense of that mess and just looked for a place to spend the night. The next day dawned bright and clear. I had not managed to see very much of KL other than the Petronas Towers, which looked like two gigantic gray corn cobs standing sentinel over the city. Still, I was glad to be on my way nevertheless. The twin towers slowly faded in the distance behind me as I returned to the North-South Expressway and continued heading north.

The loneliness of being on the road alone hit me before I reached the neighboring state of Perak. Although there was plenty of traffic, I felt isolated on my motorbike. I hadn't talked to anyone in days, not a proper conversation anyway. I didn't count talking to a worker at the gas station while filling up as having a real conversation. I didn't even have the luxury of singing along to the radio on my bike. So to combat the loneliness, I sang songs to myself. Unfortunately, the first song that popped into my head was Indonesian singer Kris Dayanti's "Menghitung Hari." The melancholy lyrics about being all alone were not the best to sing in times of loneliness though. I racked my brain for a more suitable song to sing and finally settled on Willie Nelson's "On the Road Again."

I sang to myself until the beauty of the highway distracted me from my loneliness. The road leading into Ipoh, the capital of Perak, was very scenic with jungles and limestone hills. Just before reaching Ipoh, I stopped at the Sam Poh Tong Temple. This Buddhist temple was built inside a natural limestone hill. It had a grand arched entranceway with colorful dragons that danced on the roof.

I could feel the temperature drop a few degrees as I approached the heart of the temple and walked deeper into the cave. It was serene inside the temple with its many Buddha statues. Although I don't pray regularly, I found myself praying here for a safe journey.

The gardens outside the cave were beautifully landscaped, accentuated by the limestone hills all around. There was even a garden that could only be accessed by walking through the cave and into a clearing, as if entering a magic kingdom. It was a peaceful oasis from the noise and chaos of the city just outside. There was a fish pond and another pond filled with tortoises. I had to tear myself away from the tranquility of the temple grounds to continue my journey into Ipoh, a much-hyped destination that I was excited to finally be visiting.

While in Ipoh city—labeled as "Malaysia's lesser known food capital" by *Lonely Planet*—I ate *hor fun* for lunch, a notable local dish. I slurped it up with relish. It was a most satisfying and delicious lunch.

After eating, I decided to take a detour to Menglembu, a small town southwest of Ipoh. This town is the birthplace of my favorite brand of peanuts. I know that's a funny reason to visit a place, but I had plenty of time. And since I was already in the neighborhood, why not? These days, there is little evidence of the peanut industry there. The only monument to its past peanut glory was found in a roundabout entering the town, where three gigantic peanuts—one lying on its side, one vertical and another in a half shell with its contents of two huge nuts exposed—decorated its center. Apart from that roundabout, there was not much to see in Menglembu. Still I was happy that I had made the detour. As I left Menglembu, I totally gave that town a thumbs up, mimicking the peanut brand's simple logo.

From there I headed north toward the state of Penang, reached the ferry terminal in the evening and boarded a ferry to Penang Island at dusk. In the last light of that day, the ferry cleaved through the water, leaving a trail of white foam in its wake. I could smell the salt in the air as I looked out onto the vast expanse of the darkening sea. It was a relaxing ferry ride—one that I wished would have lasted even longer. As a motorcyclist, I was parked at the front of the ferry, allowing me to see the bright lights of Penang coming ever closer as night fell.

After finding a budget hotel, I turned my attention to food. It seemed as if I spent all my time eating while I was in Penang. My meals were varied, from the *nasi kandar* with its curried chicken and okra, to the simultaneously spicy and sour *assam laksa*, which left my tongue tingling. The next day I searched for the iconic Penang *char kway teow*. The hawker grunted his acknowledgement when I ordered from him, not even looking up at me. As he cooked, I noticed that he wore safety goggles that made him look like a steampunk hero hovering over the hot wok.

After spending so much time eating, I hardly had any time to look at the beautiful architecture of the old buildings or to enjoy much of the street art. But with a full belly, I sped across the Penang Bridge and left the island behind me, bouncing rhythmically each time I crossed one of the heat expansion joints. In the bright light of day, I could see more clearly than the previous night. The bridge itself was an amazing feat of architecture, looking like something out of a dream. Crossing the bridge, I felt like I was riding across the water on a highway that snaked forever into the sea. But once I reached the mainland, I set my sights on the northern state of Kedah.

As I made my way through Kedah and approached the Thai border, I became aware of my sense of oneness with my bike. It was as if Kap Chai and I were totally connected, and we moved as one as I leaned into every turn. Perhaps it had something to do with riding the same bike solo for so long. Even the *vroom* of my bike was comforting. It wasn't the deep, signature roar of a Harley Davidson, but the sound was familiar, like talking to a close friend. The solitude didn't bother me anymore, and I started to feel very philosophical. As the gold and green paddy fields of Kedah flashed past me, I started contemplating life and the great beyond. Why were we here on earth? What was my purpose in life? Could my purpose really be to ride a motorcycle across South East Asia?

I crossed into Thailand at the Bukit Kayu Hitam crossing. I entered Sadao in Thailand with a sense of trepidation. Bombings and shootings from the separatist activities in the southern provinces of Thailand frequently make the news. Sadao is in one of the more dangerous provinces, and I didn't want to die there. It distinctly felt like I was in a different country despite the proximity to Kedah. People spoke the sing-song Thai language, unfamiliar to my ear.

I didn't get very far into Thailand, though. Kap Chai broke down in Hat Yai. It simply wouldn't start, and I didn't know what was wrong with it. Kap Chai had done well to transport me the entire length of Peninsular Malaysia without a problem. I supposed that I should have been thankful that it broke down in an urban area rather than in the middle of nowhere on a long, lonely highway. I half pushed, half dragged my motorbike to a workshop.

When I managed to get to one, the mechanic—his fingers black with grease—said to me, "สวัสดีครับ รถเป็นอะไรครับ?" Unsure how to respond, I just nodded. I didn't realize how much I missed talking to people until I couldn't due to the language barrier. Since I didn't speak any Thai, I had to do some creative miming to explain to the mechanic what had happened.

Kap Chai had been a friend to me on this journey, and I hoped it could be fixed. As I munched on a deep-fried chicken drumstick while waiting for the mechanic to work his magic, I looked at maps to plan new routes. I hoped to make it to Bangkok and then on to Cambodia before finally reaching Vietnam. Vietnam has one of the highest motorcycle ownership rates in the world, with over eighty percent of Vietnamese households owning one. In Ho Chi Minh City, where I planned to end my trip, motorbikes and scooters rule the road. I'm sure Kap Chai will feel at home there.

Flexibility Enhances the Ride
by David Andre Davison

A click of my right heel starts the engine,

My fingers grasp the throttle.

We prepare for our ride to the mountains,

My knapsack holds food and a water bottle.

Cruising through the crowded city,

People are too numerous to count.

Some sell their goods by the road,

Pesos are welcomed in any amount.

After an hour in traffic,

We leave the crowds and cars.

Driving through the small towns

With their diverse shops and bars.

The farther we venture

Into the tranquil mountains,

Our eyes are blessed

With a view of waterfall fountains.

We strip down to our suits

And slide into the crystal pool's depth.

The cool water caresses our hot skin,

Escape from reality, a pleasant concept.

It's time to head back home

And leave a bit of paradise on earth.

But my motorbike knows the way

To its small garage's berth.

It's been a brief escape from reality

On today's motorbike trip.

Like finding a desert oasis pool,

And partaking of that first delicious dip.

My passenger has been quiet

On our excursion today.

She climbs off the motorbike

With nothing to say.

I ask her what's wrong,

Why she's been quiet on our trip.

She pulls me close to her

And plants a kiss on my lip.

Her eyes say it all.

She trusts me to drive

As long as we arrive safely home

And are both still alive.

Next weekend we return

For one of our rides.

She moves toward the motorbike

Into the front of the seat she slides.

My wife's heel starts the engine,

Her fingers grasp the throttle.

She nods in my direction

As I pick up our snack and water bottle.

Today she will glide us through traffic

Out toward a place by the sea.

On the back seat of the motorbike,

A new perspective for me.

Zigzagging through Paradise
by David Andre Davison

Escaping the crowded city, leaving traffic congestion behind,

A holiday in the province will clear my weary mind.

With the wind in my face and a view of nature's best,

My wife sits behind me, her arms wrapped around my chest.

Our motorbike glides smoothly on the curving road.

Both of us lean in unison, centering the bike's load.

We pass a small farm where a buffalo pulls a plow.

A child chases after the chickens, while her mother milks a cow.

We drive along the beach where a fisherman casts his net.

I avoid the incoming tide, careful not to get my engine wet.

We stop for an early dinner before we start homeward bound.

Before we can get off our motorbike, there are children all around.

They hold out their hands and ask for pesos to buy themselves a snack.

The restaurant owner chases them away and warns them not to come

back.

We want to give them money but are told that will only bring more,

So we buy the kids some bread from the local bakery store.

On our way home, we detour down a narrow mountain trail.

The beauty is unsurpassed, but the path is a bit frail.

At the end of the day, we are in the city near our place.

It has been quite a peaceful day, but now it's back to the rat race.

You Meet the Nicest People on a Honda
by John McMahon

Some time ago in the foggy past, an old man helped me repair the punctured rear tire of the Wave 125 I was riding on trails originally created by elephants through the jungles around the Sri Na Garind reservoir in Kanchanaburi, Thailand. There were some very rough stretches—the kind of terrain that called for an enduro—but the Wave stayed true to its reputation, doggedly pushing up, over and through the inhospitable trails. When we had patched the tube, re-beaded the tire and got the wheel set with his simple tool kit, he gave the bike a loving pat and said, "Honda is our new buffalo."

I knew what he meant, that the easy to repair, go anywhere, carry an entire family, haul your goods to market Super Cub and all of its descendants are the work-horses of Asia. That this iconic bike was integral to the growth and modernization of most of the Asian peninsula. Grannies took little ones to school on them; farmers brought animals to market with them; policemen patrolled on them; people parked them in shady places on the side of the road and napped sitting on them. Whole families packed tightly rode to market or temple wearing their finery. They allow for a movable feast, carrying carts of steaming noodles, grilled chicken, donuts and anything else edible around the country. In rural areas almost every commodity or trade is practiced on the back of a motor scooter. He meant that the old Hondas were like members of the family, but ones that were always available and ready to go—night or day, rain or shine.

Any photo taken in Southeast Asia over the last 60 years would likely include a Honda Super Cub somewhere in the frame. The bikes are so ubiquitous one must take a mental leap back to an era of pre-mechanization to a time of buffalo carts and human-powered rickshaws to imagine the region without them. In the overwhelmingly agricultural countryside, most people would have gone from walking directly to riding a motorbike as bicycles were almost useless outside of big towns and cities. This was exactly the niche that the team of friends who started Honda was looking to fill. Takeo Fujisawa saw the evolution of the motor vehicle in most of the developed world as going from motorized bicycles to motorcycles to small cars and finally to larger, more expensive cars as an unrealistic model for most of Asia. Instead, he envisioned a vehicle that didn't fit into that graduated system—one that was an end unto itself.

In 1958 partners Soichiro Honda and Fujisawa released the Super Cub, a 50cc motorbike that was meant to be that end product. Honda was a performance-minded engineer who studied bikes across Europe and went to the Isle of Man TT race to watch the English and German bikes compete. It was there that he vowed to someday win the trophy, which he did in 1962 after only three years of competing. Fujisawa kept sales in mind, addressing the challenge of performance paired with ease of use. He formulated that if Honda could engineer a motorbike capable of being ridden with one hand, then he could sell it to every soba noodle shop in the country—a very modest goal in hindsight.

Small cc motorbikes at the time were little more than bicycles with clip-on engines and headlamps—a beginner's stepping stone to owning a real motorcycle. The Super Cub was specifically engineered to be a wholly different vehicle, a shift from the traditional market of men who liked to get their hands dirty to one of people with little or no mechanical know-how. Honda combined a low compression, four-stroke engine, auto-clutch and higher capacity electronics to make the bike easier to start, quieter, cooler, cleaner and, in general, *took the terror out of motorcycling.*

Its larger tires made it possible to tackle the dirt roads, mud and hills of rural Asia. The wide, lightweight plastic front fairing and conquistador-style fenders protected the rider from road debris that, along with an enclosed chain drive, kept the riders' clothes clean so that a teacher or doctor could ride one to work.

The revolutionary under-bone chassis, which came to be known as "step through," hid the engine, gas tank and all the hoses and wires that made it run. The sequential gearing made it possible to ride with open-toed shoes or no shoes at all, and the step through design made it easy to slip on and off in *longi, pa kao ban, sari* or skirt. This made it acceptable for women to ride without compromising their modesty. Possibly this design contributed to the promotion of women's rights in traditional Asian societies by giving them freedom of mobility to trade and earn money.

The design of the Super Cub was not only functional but beautiful, especially to non-motorcyclists. The profile lines of the plastic fairings ran in soft curves unlike the hard metal angles of other bikes. The two-passenger seat was larger and more comfortable than the traditional single leaf spring bicycle seats and could accommodate two, three or even four people. The front and rear drum brakes were revolutionary for the time, making the bike look and feel safe. The simple control panel with its single speedometer and thumb switches for lights made it accessible for novices to just get on and ride.

In 1960 Honda and Fujisawa opened the largest motorcycle factory in the world. Using a platform build modeled after Volkswagen's Beetle production, they were soon putting out 50,000 Honda Super Cubs a month. The bike was a clean, low-maintenance, highly functional and easy-to-ride machine that was priced for the everyman and woman. By the mid 1960s the bike was taking off, from Japan to Bangladesh and Singapore to Korea. The Super Cub changed the face of transport in Asia and then began penetrating markets in the rest of the world.

Their ingress into European and American markets was part and parcel to their overall plan of market domination. Honda knew repair and maintenance had to be readily accessible so the American Honda Company was set up in 1959 and, quickly after, a network of sales offices spread across Europe. Sales in Europe were good, but America proved a slower, more difficult prospect. Still Honda created their foothold eventually with the timeless You Meet the Nicest People on a Honda slogan to overcome the black leather jackets and violence connected to the outlaw motorcycle image that was gaining traction at the time. By the mid 1960s Honda had become integrated into middle class life. The Beach Boys wrote a song about them. Elvis Presley chased Ann Margret on one in *Viva Las Vegas*. Greg Brady rode one to school.

Anyone who has ever traveled around Asia—and especially Southeast Asia—has stories born on the back of a bike. My first moto-taxi ride in Bangkok was flying through the stalled traffic of Bang Na Trat on a Honda Wave. Weaving through the boondoggle of traffic gridlock felt dangerous. I was stunned that moto-taxi driver was an occupation and that taking one was the normal commute for many. I was even further surprised to see women riding sidesaddle on the pillion.

On one of my first trips to Koh Pang Yang Island—before it was overrun with tourists—the bartender at the Hollywood beach bar took me to my first buffalo fight on the back of his SC 90. We drank beer and his family's homemade *lao pha* with his friends all day while betting on a string of winning bulls. In the evening we rode the rutted dirt paths over the hills with the wobbly single beam of the headlight cutting the otherwise undisturbed darkness. He drunkenly dropped the bike three times, laying us out each time, but somehow we remained unscathed. When we decided to walk the rest of the way, he told the bike it was no fault of its own—that he was just too drunk. We left it in the jungle at the side of the road.

The first kayaking run I ever made on one of my favorite rivers high in the hills of Sangkhlaburi was made possible by a local Karen man and his Honda Dream. Modified with stouter shocks and knobby tires, it carried us on the rough trail and up the almost vertical hill climbs. The two of us pushed the bike through thick, red mud at the crests and fishtailed down the back side in a near freewheel. It was a dangerous but often hilarious venture with both of us and my kayak on the 110 cc machine. We arrived at the river covered in filth.

Recently in Dawai, Myanmar, I was escorted to the finer points of town by a gregarious gentleman I met in the market who wanted to show me the sights as well as show off his English. We went to the largest reclining Buddha in the nation, the university—that looked fine from a distance but proved to be only half finished and already declining—and the new mall that anticipated good fortunes owing to the construction of the largest deepwater port, gas works and possible high speed rail that would purportedly connect China to Vietnam via Myanmar and Thailand and surely destroy the natural beauty of the place in the process. For three hours we rode around town on his beautiful, vintage, sixties-era SC 90, a bike that was until recently still more a necessity than an affectation in the repressed country.

Not that many years ago, the old SC 50s 70s and 90s had a revival in Thailand. Kids were dragging the old bikes out of their grannies' back lots, cleaning them up and riding around in packs. Some restored them to their original clean and simple look, while others pimped them out or chopped them to the point where they were almost unrecognizable. It was a cool trend that seemed to be wholly original to Thailand. That trend, however, has since been more or less crushed by the newly affordable "Big Bikes" flooding the market, but there are still a few people who out there who take pride in their retro rides.

Riding on the back of a motorcycle isn't just a way to get from A to B. The proximity forces an intimacy that, in many cases, would be extremely awkward. Whether with a stranger or your sweetheart, having a rider on the pillion—where they have to wrap their arms around you and get up close to talk in your ear while you speed somewhat dangerously along—breaks the ice like nothing else.

To date there are more than 85 million Honda Super Cubs on the road. The bike changed all the rules for motorcycle builders and the face of riders the world over. It is considered the standard bearer of quality and is the most produced motor vehicle ever. There are many imitations; Honda itself has a new line of vintage SCs on the market, including the new electric EV Club. It is a bulletproof piece of engineering that, no matter what you ride—be it a full dress road hog or a balls-out street fighter—your bike owes a debt to Honda's innovation and the little Super Cub 50.

The Inner Spark
by Barry Rosenberg

Spiro was startled. *Was the plane on fire? Was it his fault?* Impossible, surely. He realized that the dancing flames were just the sun's reflection. With relief he watched as the plane descended into Denpasar's airport.

The plane taxied to a halt and, after a short delay, the doors opened. As the passengers disembarked, Spiro scanned their faces as they passed by. His own face lit up with delight when he spotted his wife Ada, a tall woman with a mop of ginger hair. Seeing him, she waved and hurried toward the arrivals lounge. They met and embraced.

Separating, Spiro asked, "How was the expo?"

"Pretty good. There are heaps of expats in Surabaya."

"Do they speak Indonesian?"

Ada waved her hand in a yes-no manner. "Some, yes, but they can't do web design."

Spiro collected two bags from the carousel. "So we still corner the expat market in web design. Good. And the flight?"

"It was fine."

Ada, unusually quiet, picked up the second case and quickened her pace to keep up with her husband. Both were fit as they surfed several times a week. During the rains, they went to the gym.

Leaving the terminal, she inhaled. "Flowers and spices and clove cigarettes." Ada took another deep breath. "Bali must have the best smelling airport in the world."

"The best smelling surrounds, anyway." Spiro led the way to a motorbike with an attached sidecar. Once smooth and gleaming black, in true Balinese fashion, it was now decorated with bumps and scratches. Patting the sides affectionately, Spiro put the cases in the sidecar and then mounted the bike. Ada sat behind with her arms around his waist.

Usually when on the bike, Ada would shout comments into Spiro's ear. Today, however, she still remained unusually quiet. When they stopped at traffic lights, Spiro turned and asked, "Is everything okay?"

Ada adjusted the helmet so her hair fit better. "Yes, I guess." But at the next stop she added, "I'm not really sure. There was this Aussie bloke, Liam Waverly, at the expo. He kept asking me out." She sighed. "He wouldn't take no for an answer and so one evening I went for a drink with him. Big mistake. He became even pushier after that."

"He knew you were married?"

"No problem for him."

"Well," Spiro angrily stamped his foot down, accelerating sharply, "it's a good thing he's in Surabaya, and we're in Ubud."

"Yes." Ada closed her eyes and clung tighter. "A good thing."

She was glad to be going home to their house in Ubud overlooking the rice fields. Although they were computer people, they enjoyed living in a town known for its artists and eccentric expats. Nearing its outskirts, her tension lessened while Spiro drove more carefully in the crazy Balinese traffic.

It was winter dark when they arrived—dark enough for Spiro to concentrate until, one by one, he had lit half a dozen oil lamps. "That's more romantic." He grinned.

Rubbing her arms after an hour on the back of the motorbike, Ada slowly began to undo her blouse. "A week away. I could do with some romance."

Her top open, she pressed her breasts against his chest. Spiro bent to kiss her, and she tightly wrapped herself around him. At the end of their love-making, Spiro knew better than to speak. But he intuitively understood that although his wife was strong and brave, the bloke at the expo had really unsettled her.

They stayed on the living room floor, the oil lamps creating a cozy atmosphere. Eventually, however, Spiro rose. "I've made dinner. But first ..." He reached behind a settee and produced a bunch of roses.

"How lovely!" Ada clasped them to her chest. "Beautiful."

"And the finest candle that money can buy."

Spiro brought out a candle carved into the shape of a lotus. Putting it on the table, he concentrated on it for a few moments. The wick began to smolder. With extra concentration on his part, the wick burst into flame. Just as the oil lamps had done when they'd first returned home. Ada watched with delight but said nothing. She was well accustomed to her husband's unusual ability.

Liam Waverly's house in Surabaya was built with high walls surrounding it. Their purpose was to hide his shooting range from his neighbors. Target practice in the back garden was, of course, illegal. His owning of a handgun was illegal and so was its use with a silencer. But Liam took photos in the wild. Because of that, he believed that he needed a weapon and wanted to be well-rehearsed in its use. Being generous with his money had also helped when the authorities stopped by and questioned him about it.

He stood with his arms hanging loosely and a deep frown upon his rugged face. The photographer was thinking ... brooding.

That woman. She'd led me on. Every day, she'd been at the expo, obviously waiting for me. She'd even gone out for a drink with me. She'd hardly mentioned her husband. Obviously, she was besotted with me. He lightly touched the pistol in his pocket. *We were meant be together.*

In one swift motion, Liam drew his small handgun. Pausing for a moment, his fingers caressed the curved walnut stock. Then he sighted along the metal barrel and pulled the trigger. The hammer snapped forward, and the pin struck the primer. Creating a spark, it ignited the gunpowder. With the resulting explosion, the bullet shot out of the barrel and hit the target. The photographer strolled forward and grunted with satisfaction. *Not bad at thirty paces for a tiddly Smith & Wesson. Not too bad, at all.*

Liam returned to the firing line and prepared to fire again. But his thoughts made him restless. *That woman!* Putting on the safety switch, he slipped the pistol back into his jacket. Then, much to the relief of his neighbors, he turned off the spotlights used to illuminate his backyard.

Back in his bungalow, the photographer looked at his work schedule. He looked directly at it but didn't see it. His thoughts had switched again to *that woman. Yes, it was time to act.* He folded up his job sheets. *Some things, you just have to fight for.* Liam sat down and poured himself rum. It slid down smoothly, and he poured himself another. Sipping on this second glass more slowly, he decided that he would go to bed soon. He wanted to be up early to sort out his business with the wildlife magazine, Then he wanted to finalize a plan to deal with *that woman.*

The next morning after an early bacon and egg breakfast, Liam picked up his phone and dialed *Indonesian Wildlife*. When no one answered his call, he growled. "Lazy buggers! Why isn't anyone there yet?" He knew it was too early for anyone to be at work, but his impatience made him blind to any plans but his own. On his fifth try, he got through. "Get me Dr. Dasai," he snapped. When the magazine publisher took the call, Liam didn't allow him to speak but verbally bombarded him. "I emailed the first set of photos to your department. I haven't heard back from them yet, so there'll be a delay in reworking them. I'll get back to you when the project is complete."

He slammed the phone down. The delay had actually been his. After seeing Ada, he'd forgotten to email the photos. *Ah well, such is life.* He then went into the garage and considered his two vehicles. One was a sleek and bright yellow sports car that he used it when he went into town and wanted to impress the girls.

The other vehicle was a four wheel drive with high wheels. Solidly built, it was excellent for tracking animals along muddy roads and crossing swollen creeks. He nodded. Clearly, the 4WD was what he needed for driving to Bali, a ten-hour trip, which *that woman* had flown in a comfortable hour.

Making sure that his pistol was loaded, Liam slid it into his jacket pocket. Loading up the 4WD, he stroked his thin moustache and started the engine. The motor turned over, and he set off. By that evening the exhausted photographer had reached Ubud. After checking into a hotel, he considered ordering a masseuse before deciding that it would be better to get a full night's rest instead. Although Ada wanted him to rescue her, there could be trouble with her husband.

The next morning Spiro awoke with his wife nestled against him. Because the heavy drapes darkened the room, he concentrated on the nearest oil lamp. The wick flickered, flared, and the oil lamp threw a gentle light across the bedroom.

Ada raised her head. "Can you do anything else with that ... talent of yours?"

"I can start a cigarette lighter or any small fire, I guess."

Ada purred. "Baby, can you light my fire?" She rolled on top of him. "Are you concentrating? I think I'm getting warm."

This was a playful lovemaking, different from the edginess of the night before. Spiro was pleased. His wife had shaken off her fears.

After breakfast, Ada went into her workshop. Her husband followed her.

"What're you working on?" he asked.

"A wooden automata." Ada presented a small wooden box with a carved hunter and kangaroo on its top. When she turned the handle, cams inside the box caused the hunter to lift up his rifle. At the same time, gears caused the kangaroo to jump from side to side. The automata gave the impression that whenever the hunter fired, the kangaroo hopped out of the line of sight.

"That's great!" Spiro exclaimed.

"Not quite. See?" The mechanism jerked. "The gears are a bit sticky. I need a finer file." She put the box down. "I'll just nip out and buy one."

After kissing her husband, Ada removed her apron and left the house. Although they were in a quiet area, there were still plenty of *bemos* chugging past. It was easy for her to flag one down.

Once inside, the other passengers asked the typical range of questions that foreigners receive. *How old are you? Where are you from? How many children have you got?*

As they chatted Ada admired the lush, green countryside on either side of the road. She was also aware of the women wearing bright *sarongs* as they walked along the street with baskets on their heads. She didn't, however, notice the 4WD that followed the *bemo*. Nor did she take any notice of it when it stopped outside the hardware shop. Looking forward to buying another file, she entered the store. Recognizing her, several of the assistants greeted her with a traditional bow with their palms pressed together.

Pleased at being acknowledged, Ada greeted the assistants by name. Then, selecting a file, she paid and left. Once back in the street, she decided to visit her favorite coffee house. As well as having delicious cakes, it had a spectacular view over the surrounding fields, the view enhanced by the magical tinkle of *gamelan* music. Walking with anticipation, it never occurred to her to look behind. Consequently, she jumped when a heavy hand landed on her shoulder.

"You wanted me to come, and so I came."

Ada stared at Liam, her eyes big with surprise. "I ... I didn't want you to come here, and I'll be very pleased to see you go."

"Nah, you're just saying that. You like to put up a challenge."

His hand still resting on her shoulder, he tried to bring her toward him. Without thinking, Ada swung the metal file.

"Bloody hell!" Liam shouted as it connected with his hand. "But I see you're playing hard to get."

"You leave me alone!"

The passers-by paused on seeing the couple argue, and the driver of a *bemo* looked like he might intervene. The photographer stepped back, spreading his arms as if to show he was harmless. Now, however, Ada was too upset to go to the coffee shop. She stopped another *bemo* and, this time, didn't say another word to the other passengers. Ada managed not to cry until she made it back at home. She ran into Spiro's arms.

"That madman is here! Liam Waverly—from the expo. The one who won't take no for an answer."

Spiro held his wife, stroking her back and making soothing noises. Eventually, her cries faded, and she wiped her eyes. "We should tell the police," he said.

Ada shook her head. "But there's nothing they can do. He'll say he's here because I wanted him to come. It's just his word against mine."

Spiro exhaled deeply. "In that case, while he's here, we'd better stick together."

Ada looked sadly at her husband. "Perhaps he'll leave sooner if we don't go out."

But that was impossible. That very day, Spiro needed to post his mother's birthday present to Brisbane. In the afternoon when he'd finally wrapped it, he waved the parcel in the air. "Ada, we can't bury ourselves. We have to go to the post office."

His wife sighed. "So it's come to this. We're in beautiful Bali, and that bloke acts as if we're still in the Stone age."

Spiro led the way into their bamboo garage. Putting his parcel into the motorbike's sidecar, he sat on the bike and turned to her. "Look what I can do now." He concentrated. Suddenly the engine coughed. Spiro tapped the accelerator and the motorbike roared. He grinned. "Hows about that?"

"Good, very good."

Ada also grinned, but it was obvious that she was too distracted to be impressed with Spiro's expanding abilities. As they headed down the main road, Liam followed from a distance. This time, however, Ada was watching out for him. She leaned forward and shouted, "He's following us."

Spiro's expression tightened. "Good. I'll go and ask him what the hell he thinks he's doing."

"No, don't! He could become violent."

Spiro stopped the bike and jutted his chin toward the street. "Too many people around. Surely, he wouldn't cause trouble in front of so many witnesses."

As he walked toward the other vehicle, Spiro's vision tunneled, the other people and the street dropping away. There was just him and the man stalking his wife. A cold anger grew inside him, and his fists clenched. The passers-by stopped. They recognized that walk.

The photographer sat in his 4WD and waited. His hand rested on his jacket pocket, the pistol a comfort. If her *so-called* husband attacked with so many people around serving as witnesses, he could easily shoot him in self-defense. *So let him come.* Liam would do his best to provoke him.

"Mr. Waverly." Spiro was used to running his eye over lines of code, a skill that he brought to all difficult situations. So when he saw the other man run his hand over his pocket, he was shocked to make out the outline of a pistol. He slowly unclenched his fists. This man was obviously beyond argument. "My wife and I are happily married. She is not at all interested in your intentions."

Liam had the sudden urge to push his door open and knock the young fool down. But he controlled the impulse, instead transforming the physical act into the cold ferocity of his voice. "She is merely under your thumb. If you were out of the way, then she would be free to be with me."

Moving beyond the reach of the door, Spiro's mind rapidly ticked over. With the ghost of an idea beginning to take form, he made his tone as contemptuously challenging as possible. "Then come and get her," he snapped.

Liam punched the steering wheel. "Don't worry, I will. I know where you live," he said, his flat tone more chilling than shouting.

"That won't be of much help." Spiro turned away. "Tomorrow, we leave town on business."

Liam glared. "*You* would do well to leave earlier."

Spiro shrugged as if he didn't feel threatened. "I have work to finish, and you aren't going to stop me."

Trying to appear casual, he returned to the motorbike. The street came alive again and the onlookers continued on their way. Ada studied her husband. His face was set in a way she'd never seen before.

"What?" she asked.

"He's obsessed. He really means trouble."

"Can we tell the police now?"

Spiro shook his head. "He still hasn't done anything. There's nothing they can do."

"But we must do something!" Ada's voice rose in a wail.

"I'm already onto it." Spiro put his hand on her arm and gazed at her with affection. "Don't worry. We'll get out of this."

Ada smiled sadly. "Don't worry? But we've never been in a situation like this before."

With the engine off, Spiro once again concentrated on the ignition. Now, on this second time, his anger caused the engine to roar into life. The bike started, and they remained silent but wary as they continued to the post office. Spiro was careful to park by the entrance when they arrived.

"Stay by the door and keep an eye on the bike," he said. "Make sure that bugger doesn't try anything."

Ada nodded, and Spiro joined the back of the line to send his parcel. As he waited, he made a phone call, keeping his voice low so that Ada couldn't hear him. He didn't want to worry her.

After finishing up at the post office, Spiro and Ada got back on their bike. He could feel her tense hold around his waist as she sat behind him. He gazed upward into the blue sky. Under such a sky, he thought, one should be happy.

"Before we go home," he said over his left shoulder, "let's go to the Water Palace."

Nodding her agreement, Ada bumped her chin on her husband's shoulder. It wasn't far to the palace. It was just a little difficult to find as it was hidden behind coffee shops and restaurants. Spiro, however, had no problem in finding his way as this was a place that they often went to relax. For them, the main draw was the pond at the front. This was fed by water from the temple and overflowed with pink blossoms, rising from wide green lotus leaves. They wandered around the temple, letting its calm sink into them. Spiro breathed deeply. Even the air here seemed cleaner.

Ada kissed Spiro on the cheek. "Thank you. I feel much better now."

Spiro could feel the difference when his wife was again on the back of the motorbike. Instead of clutching him around the waist, her touch was more of a caress. He, too, was more relaxed, and he started the motorbike with just a touch of his mind. They arrived home and Ada went into her workshop to use her new file.

Spiro went to his computer and tried to work on a website. But having told Waverly that they were going away the next morning, he expected trouble before that—most probably after dark. He looked at the time—two more hours to sunset. He set a timer and then placed an unlit candle behind him before returning to work on the website. This time, he became so absorbed that when the timer shrilled, he jumped. He had difficulty remembering why he had set it in the first place. Focusing on the candle, his agitation caused it to immediately burst into flame.

He continued working on the computer for another hour, resetting the timer and mentally lighting the candle. But he decided he needed a test that was a little more machinelike. He went outside and sat on the motorbike. He concentrated, but the engine didn't start. He worked to empty his mind while simultaneously filling it with intention. He tried again. On this second attempt, the engine started. He slid backward onto the back seat. Again, he practiced until he could mentally fire up the motorbike, continuing until he felt exhausted.

A little before sunset, Spiro made another phone call. *Yes, his earlier message had been received, and they were making further investigations.* He had done all he could do in pursuing that avenue. He went into Ada's workshop.

She held up a large gear. "I'm giving the teeth an angle. That should make them run smoother."

"It's getting dark." Spiro held out his hand. "Let's go into the living room."

They entered the house, leaving the front door unlocked. Spiro didn't switch on the electric lights but only lit the oil lamps. Ada sat by a lamp and tried to read. The web designer shuffled a deck of cards and played pretence.

Ada suddenly looked up. "Did a shadow just pass the window?"

"I hope so," Spiro replied. "At least, I think I hope so."

"You're expecting him to come?"

"More than expecting." Spiro dropped a handful of cards. "I invited him."

It was dark outside. Lights were on in nearby houses, and cars zoomed along the main road. They pretended to be occupied when all they were doing was waiting ... just waiting. Before too long, they picked up the faint sound of someone trying very hard to be stealthy.

Spiro called out, "Come on in. The door isn't locked."

A burly shadow suddenly filled the doorway. "You think you're being clever." It was Liam's rough growl. He stepped into the room. "Anyone else here?" He cocked his head, listening and looking.

"No."

He laughed. "That's 'cause you really didn't think I'd come." Swiftly, he drew out his pistol. "Let her go, or I'll give her no reason to stay."

Spiro gulped. He couldn't believe that a gun was being pointed at him. He tried to concentrate as he had with the motorbike. But the black hole of the barrel was an abyss into which his focus fell.

"You wouldn't dare," he muttered, finding it difficult to dredge up the words.

"I have and would again."

For the second time, Spiro tried to concentrate. Not succeeding, he said, "Ask Ada if she wants to go."

"You've hypnotized her so that she doesn't know her own mind."

Liam curled his finger a little tighter around the trigger. Sweating, Spiro tried for the third time.

Suddenly, Ada darted in front of her husband. "You'll have to shoot me first."

With Ada blocking him, Liam's hand started to drop. Immediately, Spiro's mind relaxed. Then it reached out and touched the pistol. To Liam's surprise, even though he held the trigger loosely, the pistol fired. The bullet skimmed his trousers, tore his boot, and embedded itself in the wooden floor.

While the shot was still reverberating, a tall figure burst into the room. Wearing a policeman's uniform. He swung his baton. There was a sharp snap as something broke, and the pistol dropped to the floor.

The photographer screamed. "You broke my bloody arm."

"I'll break a lot more if you don't come quietly." The policeman put handcuffs on Liam. "After your message, sir," he said in Indonesian, "we rang Surabaya. There have been other complaints about Mr. Waverly, but none that could be substantiated. Well, we've got him now. I heard everything he said, and I saw him fire his pistol." The policeman paused. "Lucky for you, he fired when he was letting down his aim."

Ada and Spiro exchanged glances. "Yes," they said, "luckily for us."

Then, while gazing behind the policeman, Spiro caused an oil lamp to slowly come alight.

The Great, All-Night Khaosan Road Bike Race
by Charlie Baylis

Gasoline drips from my dream,

the hymn that my wheels sing,

racing down Khaosan Road.

Here is a future I'll leave behind

my motorbike takes off and the sun whacks out

the wings on the biker's backs.

Don't tell me about your lost paradise.

My paradise: *found*. I chance a right, zoom

round the gold dipped temples, the monks are heading

home to hold their daughters. The petals

of my milk filled frame smash

into concrete walls in an orange boom.

By nightfall the riders are all dressed in black,

their lungs are bust, their tongues are blue.

The sweat of soft leather sweetens

on trips to heaven, the bikers' love

left

spinning in the oil rainbows on the road.

There are signs

they lead to higher places.

Old Soldier
by Michael Lund

Manfred didn't know exactly why he decided to go back to Vietnam forty-five years after he'd left. "Just to see," he told his wife with a faraway look. To Jackson, his remaining brother, he offered, "For closure." With his children, who'd never quite understood his role over there, he grew philosophical: "Maybe I want to see a new country, post-American—or the old one, pre-American." But it probably had as much to do with the discovery that he was an "old soldier." He'd never accepted the fact that he'd been a young one.

He had resurrected—if that's the right word—the term "old soldier" a year ago when he drove from St. Louis to Fairfield to attend his fiftieth high school reunion. Passing the exit for St. James, a town of several thousand ten miles east of his home, he felt an image rise up from his childhood memories: the Old Soldiers Home up on a hill dotted with trees and brick walkways. On family trips, sitting between his younger sister and older brother in the back seat of the family's 1955 Nash Ambassador, he had seen the red stone structure many times and wondered vaguely who resided in such a facility. He now asked himself, if the institution existed today, would he qualify?

Almost half a century earlier, after eight weeks of easily forgotten basic training, Manfred had spent nine months of 1969 in the collegiate atmosphere of the Army's language school in Fort Ord, California. Then, when he was assigned as a military liaison for the University of Maryland's extension program in Saigon, rather than be sent into the bush, he felt an odd sense of continuity between his civilian life before he'd been drafted and the military life that followed.

"I've gone back to Central High School," he wrote his sister back in the Show Me State; she was studying to be a high school teacher. "But now, instead of being a student, I'm the guidance counselor." His assignment was to assist career soldiers wanting to get college credit for military training and experience. He was not, then, he concluded to himself with a certain satisfaction, a "soldier."

At the insistence of others in his basic training company, the Army had taken note of the teaching degree he'd earned at Northwestern and kept him out of the infantry. The same powers that be had also come to see that the Vietnamese learned English faster than Army recruits mastered their native language; so there was less need for American translators than expected. As a result Manny maintained an academic identity throughout most of his two-year enlistment, going to classes himself and then conducting advising sessions for another body of students.

Almost half a century later the rush of heat outside the Tan Son Nhat International Airport terminal robbed the retired school superintendent of his breath and his composure. It was the same as in 1970 when, with several hundred other men, he'd stepped down from a chartered jet transport onto the runway tarmac at Cam Ranh Bay. In 2015 he felt for the first time that his life might, in fact, be bracketed by before and after Vietnam. He was at once an old soldier and the young one he'd never acknowledged.

In addition to climate, the traffic drew him back to the world he and three other enlisted men had encountered outside the compound, a former French villa where they'd lived and worked. Hundreds of bicycles, compact cars, motor scooters and rickshaws swarmed around buses and small trucks in streets, alleyways and even sidewalks. Inside a cab on the way to his hotel Manfred studied vehicles and their passengers, but he also remembered a moment when he'd been on the back of a motorbike, comfortably (but uncomfortably) sandwiched between two young women. "What am I doing here?" he'd asked then. He asked it again now.

The sounds of cars and trucks—backfires (that before could have been gunfire) and horns (that might have been alerts)—shouts of drivers and pedestrians (Manny couldn't catch a word in the language he'd once studied), construction equipment (street level and above), music from stores created a confusion similar to what he'd felt as he rode in a Jeep, the Center's NCO at the wheel, barreling from in-country processing to his new post.

"You are a former soldier, G.I.?" the cab driver inquired.

"Well, 'soldier,' ... " he hesitated. "I was, um, here as part of an American university educational program."

He had dodged his first confrontation, but the subtle disorientation of travel was preparing him for more.

As he was filling out the hotel's registration form, he inquired about walking tours of the former Saigon. "Mr. Tri will know," the young woman smiled, gesturing toward a desk at the entrance.

Keys in hand, Manny inspected the brochures laid out on the concierge's desk. "We have many guests like you," said the man he assumed to be Mr. Tri, a handsome man perhaps as old as himself.

"Like me? You mean, Americans?"

"Yes, those who have been here before. Usually you want to go into the countryside. It is beautiful in so many places of our nation."

"I'm sure it is, but I spent my year ... my time in Sai ... when I was here ... in Ho Chi Minh City." He hesitated. "I might, though, go for a few days down to Vung Tau, the Delta."

One of his friends from Fort Ord had been stationed at a language school in that former French resort town, and Manny had been mildly irritated that Benjamin's assignment matched his training. Studying up for this trip, Manny had read that the old school building, close to the South China Sea, had at one time been converted to a B&B and thought perhaps it would be fitting if he tried to find it as a part of his ... of what? ... his pilgrimage?

"That, too, is a beautiful city," agreed the concierge. "May I inquire if you need guides for your visit? I see you are not with a group, and I can tell you that visitors find driving here difficult." He gestured through the hotel doors at the stream of traffic. "The streets are not well marked for foreigners."

Manny remembered watching from behind the security fence topped with concertina wire as pedestrians passed his education center— young girls in white *áo dàis* on their way to and from Catholic schools; street vendors hawking fish, meat and vegetables; laborers carrying bricks or sand or water in buckets at the ends of shoulder yokes; women with laundry stacked high above their heads. It had been one of his recreations in slow times, but he was too often pulled out of that reverie by the guards who scanned traffic for selfish reasons more than security.

"That guy right there," Wilson would point, nudging Manny with an elbow. "He's got good dope in his pack. And he pimps for the whorehouse down the street. You ought to go there sometime, Little Man." Wilson nicknamed everyone, using an indecipherable personal code. Manny, center on his high school basketball team, was slender, but over six feet tall.

The education unit's guards came from Military Assistance Command (MAC-V), headquarters for all in-country U.S. forces. Two were on duty flanking the gate during daylight hours and two more manned corner watchtowers at night. Most had rotated out of the field, having survived enough combat to deserve time in the rear at the end of their tours.

"I hope to find the place where I ... lived." He almost said to the concierge "where I was stationed." He went on. "Is there anyone who would remember that time ... 1970, it was."

The man smiled. "I will be that man." He bowed. "Trong Tri at your service."

Manny thought his smile was strained but, given his position at the hotel, assumed the concierge would be reliable. A time was set for a tour of the area on the second full day of his visit. He'd decided to rest after the long flight and enjoy the hotel amenities before then, including the art of a Chinese masseuse. He'd read about hot stone massages, warmth pressing you into a thin firm mattress on a portable table. And then he would book a bus tour to Vung Tau.

Trying to go to sleep that first night, restless from jet lag, he conjured up childhood images of aging pensioners in the Missouri Old Soldiers' Home—broken, bent, drooling figures mumbling about long ago wartime experiences. When he rose after fitful sleep, wedged between the wall and a row of pillows, he examined himself in the mirror.

Scanning a row of books available for reading in the hotel lobby after breakfast, he recalled one of the trivial events that had characterized his duties. "Bookends, for God's sake," he'd exploded about a month into his tour. The university catalogs had tumbled from the shelf above his desk for a second time that morning. "Why the hell can't we get something as simple as metal fucking bookends?"

The office stocked catalogs from many universities in order to determine which courses would transfer to Maryland and what classes would satisfy requirements in existing programs. They also had publications from accrediting agencies in the States.

He researched the process of ordering supplies and put in a requisition to Staff Sergeant Topp. "All I want," he'd said irritably, "is two standard metal bookends—a vertical plate anchored to a horizontal base, an L-shape. One at this end of my shelf, a second at the other, clamping our books together so they don't spill out onto the floor."

"Any chance you're taking this too serious, Specialist?" Sgt. Topp asked, looking up from his desk. "We *are* in a war zone."

"No ... no, Sergeant, I don't believe so. Just want things to be a bit more orderly."

"All in a row, then?"

"Exactly."

The form left, but the bookends never came. Wilson said he was way too uptight and produced a second nickname: "Buttoned," pronouncing it more as "butt-ended."

Wilson also kept after him about visiting Madame Kim-Ly's. "You can get anything you want there, Buttoned Man—I mean *anything*." He had a conspicuous gap between his two front teeth, and Manfred felt that alone squeezed his speech into indecencies.

To turn the question away, Manny asked, "What do *you* ask for?"

"Oh, it's different every time, but ... " he leaned into Manny, whose other shoulder was pressed against the guard box. "But what you should try is a shower with two girls. One in front, one behind."

Manny, curious in an intellectual way, couldn't figure what the second girl would be doing. "What if I just wanted to talk? Learn about her, her family, life before the war, her hopes for the future."

Wilson laughed. "That's a good one. I might even try that as a kind of prelude, know what I mean? And we could take it up again later. A long night with before, during and afters."

Trong Tri could find the street where Manfred's education center had been located, but so much was changed that nothing recalled the year 1970. "I remember it as a pretty standard colonial structure," he mused. "It would be a shame if it was destroyed. Yellow concrete walls, tiled wall mosaics, a small arcade. Just two stories, but large rooms, wide windows."

The windows had been shuttered, but at night with the lights out he could part them in the middle and look out at the busy city. By this time in the war, most of Saigon was considered secure.

"You see," Trong Tri observed, "this was where many refugees from the country came during the American War." Manny had learned that was their term for the conflict. "It has all been changed. No more shacks made from flattened Budweiser cans, no cardboard box homes, tarps spread over packing crates."

"I remember seeing them," admitted Manny.

Trong Tri's face did not change, but he said, "I lived there, perhaps close to the place we are standing."

Manny felt an obligation to inquire. "You and your family came from ..."

"Tây Nguyên, which you called the Highlands, many generations. But we were driven south. And then, about the time you were here, your people pressed us to go back. You claimed it was safe now, peace was being restored; but we knew that was not true. How do you say it? We were 'between a rock and a hard place'?"

"I remember something like that," Manny admitted. On the Armed Forces Radio Network he had heard stories about pacification, return to normalcy. The U.S. would leave soon, the people were told, and a stable democracy would remain. The refugees should go back to their villages.

"We were ..." Trong Tri looked around, as if it might be dangerous to say too much about those times. "Now we see that we were being pressed between two giant forces, Capitalism and Communism, when all we wanted to do was live as our ancestors had for thousands of years."

Manny suggested they go back to the hotel. He didn't want to know more about this man's history.

His Army job had been to connect military experience to civilian training, giving soldiers a complete transcript. With his help they might get promotions within the service or take up new careers outside the military. Was Trong Tri's present a continuation of his past? Had anyone helped him link pre-war to post-war, or had his identity been destroyed in the gap?

The tour bus to Vung Tau was perhaps the most luxurious he'd ever ridden in with its air-conditioning, satellite reception and plush reclining seats. And the sights along the way were spectacular, beginning with the Cai Be, a colorful floating wholesale market that sits on the waters of the Mekong River. At stops along the way he learned about centuries-old techniques of producing rice paper, coconut candy and fish sauce. The hotel on the beach was a four-star establishment.

Trong Tri had given him the name of his cousin, who could locate the old school, if it existed. Chien, too, was a hotel concierge, though not where Manny was staying. Still, he agreed to be a guide for an afternoon.

As they walked together, Manny thought to ask how he and his cousin had become concierges. "When we were young," explained Chien, "we learned many languages, including French, Chinese and English. At times we were translators. We learned how to conduct ourselves with different kinds of people."

"That makes sense. So you've adapted to each new situation?"

Chien paused. "Not to all, of course. We were a country at war, you know, and sometimes the war defines you."

Manny resisted that idea, still thinking he'd never been a young soldier. He didn't believe Benjamin, his classmate, had been one either ... until the end. The draft had interrupted Benny's graduate career at the University of Pennsylvania, but he planned to pick up his academic life when he returned.

Chien added. "War changes the land and buildings, too. But this could be what you're looking for."

Manny saw a long low concrete building with covered walkways and a central patio. He couldn't be sure, but his memory held up an image he could overlay on what he saw. Maybe ...

Manny had spent a night with Benny here (or at a place like here) when he'd been on R&R in Vung Tau. He was surprised to learn how seriously his friend took his assignment, giving young Vietnamese tools he felt would serve them in the post-war world. At the quiet restaurant Benny took him to, Manny had tried to revive his training, ordering in Vietnamese. Benny had to help, but the waitress seemed pleased at his effort.

For the rest of his R&R he stayed in a hotel that catered to G.I.'s and was close to several of the houses Wilson's counterpart in Vung Tau would have frequented. Manny's wild motorbike ride had been at dawn from the Saigon Sisters back to the Lotus House.

He'd had too much to drink through the night and didn't want to walk back to his hotel. "I take you, Mr. Soldier," said one of the girls and pulled him by his elbow to a moped parked by the street. "Get on behind me."

He swung a leg over and put his arms around her waist. "You're a good driver?" he worried.

"Sure thing, G.I." She revved the engine, which already seemed to have warmed the seat between his legs.

She turned the handlebar and was starting to pull into the street when Manny felt someone climb on behind him, arms tight around his chest.

"Hey!" he cried.

"Okay, G.I., okay," said a female voice in his ear. "I need ride, too." She called out something to the other girl, but Manny couldn't make out what she said.

They pulled away from the building and began weaving through traffic, headed away from the beach and his hotel. "Where're you going?" he shouted into the driver's hair. He'd heard stories of American soldiers delivered to the enemy by Vietnamese prostitutes.

She turned her head slightly to the side. "Take girl to the doctor. We must have check-ups every week. Everything fine, no worry."

The girl behind him said, "Broad shoulders. You big man, Troop." He could feel her mouth on his ear.

They drove on recklessly, Manny thought. He felt he was watching an action movie too close to the screen, images of buildings, vehicles, pedestrians streaming past him. The only good thing was that it was unlikely he'd fall off, pressed as he was between these two women.

They stopped at a pharmacy, and the girl behind him hopped off and went in a door on the side of the building. The driver leaned back into Manny, saying, "One minute, G.I. Then my turn."

Manny had no idea where he was and no recourse but to wait. Moments later, the girl emerged, and the driver went in. Rather than sit behind him, though, the second girl swung a leg across in front of him and straddled the seat.

When the first driver came out, she climbed up behind Manny. Again, they sandwiched him tightly. He'd begun to sober up, and the pressure of their bodies made him self-conscious. As they sped away, he felt people were staring at the tall American who didn't know where his hands should be.

Shouting back and forth around Manny all the way, the girls delivered him safely to Lotus House. "You come to Saigon Sisters tomorrow. You can have us both, okay?" But the next night he went to a different house and asked for only one girl.

A month later he learned that his friend Benny, recruiting potential translators in a village in the Delta, had been killed. Resistance to Americanization was often hidden, but such incidents revealed the depth of the people's resentment.

Back in Ho Chi Minh City after the excursion to Vung Tau, Manny wondered if he hadn't done what Wilson told him to do after all. Forty-five years earlier Americans had been using the men and women of this country for their own ends—some knowing full well that was the case, others naively believing they were doing good.

He'd played a small role, Manny thought, more civilian than military. Still, he'd added his abilities to a process that failed at a high cost to others. An old soldier now, he could conceive of no way to redeem the past in which he'd been a young soldier.

Rice
by Scott Reel

With a bag of rice on the back of his motorbike,

he bent around a cow in the middle of the street.

Winding over a dirt road beneath the trees,

trundling toward a penniless castle,

his sunburnt skin flashed between the virid leaves,

pressing deeper under the sun, against the breeze.

Huddling in shoeless factions,

with hot, taut black hair and brown necks,

they turned to scan the inflating sound.

Dirt-stained, pale-bottomed feet flattened—

someone from the direction of town—

but no one smiled. They panted. They stood

in the sultry shadows, capes of the gray stones

stacked high into the cloudless sky—home.

A white face. Bare arms. A shining chest. Hair

cut with a razor. A smooth chin. Two pieces of metal

dangling beneath his neck. He killed

the motor and stood. They stood together,

in the sultry shadows, draped off the gray stones

stacked high into the cloudless sky.

Two boys,

soil-colored and barefooted, froze

at attention, one wearing a badged hat,

glinting next to a stiff hand, his elbow

broken perfectly at a saluting angle.

Slowly,

the man's hand rose, his heels

forced together in the dirt,

answering the familiar welcome

in the foreign place.

His cheeks stretched,

and smiles bloomed

like flashes of camera light

in the quiet, Cambodian afternoon.

The Path of the Ghosts
by Tilon Sagulu

"Wait up, stop! Jesse! Please ... stop!" April cried, gasping for air. They were 3,400 meters above sea level. The air was so thin despite the refreshing, cool breeze. "I can't do this anymore," said April, sitting down.

It was dark. The sound of rocks grinding the boots of the climbers was loud. Jesse was relying on the light from the headlamp strapped on April's forehead, which was now pointing at a mossy rock—highlighting the greens against the gray. The soft reflection exposed the lining of April's face—bitter, hiding quietly in the shadow. It was her fault, Jesse thought. He had told April many times to train before hiking Mount Kinabalu, but she refused—always the stubborn one ever since they were kids.

"Bah, let's go," Jesse said after a minute of rest. "April, let's go! We need to get going. If we don't reach the checkpoint before 4am, we can't continue climbing the peak."

"I know lah bah!" April snapped. "Do you really have to remind me every minute?" She stood up. There was heaviness in her movement—her elephant thighs stomped as her arms and shoulders hung loose like jellyfish. Then she stopped, head lifted up into the starry sky. The headlamp cut through the thin fog. Her shoulders shuddered for a long time. Nobody knew why April cried so suddenly, but Jesse had a theory.

The night before they started hiking, they stayed at a cheap hostel in Kundasang. It was a cold, misty night, and both of them had trouble sleeping. Perhaps Jesse was too excited, but for April, she had always found it difficult to sleep in a new environment ever since she was young.

"Why did I marry him, Jesse?" April said softly as though whispering, and then sipped her chamomile tea. They were sitting on the balcony floor with wool blankets keeping them warm, facing Mount Kinabalu.

"Randy?" asked Jesse. "I don't know." He recalled that morning when he woke up early, finding his father sitting next to April. Her eyes were blood-shot and swollen, and the word "divorce" lingered in the air.

"It's Mama ... if only—" she stopped and sighed.

"What? If only what?"

"Hm?" April turned, eyebrows knotted. "What?"

"If only what?"

"Oh, nothing," she smiled and made her eyes big at Jesse. "How come everything goes so easily for you?"

"What do you mean easy?"

"You do anything you want, and Mama will always be on your side."

"Well, not *all* the time," Jesse paused. "Are you angry at her?"

"Who? Mama? No lah ... maybe I am, but I can't."

"And why is that?"

"Because she's our *mother* ..." She sipped her tea. "I mean, why can't she leave us alone? We're both adults. I'm twenty-six and you're twenty-three, but still ... she treats us like little kids. I don't know ... do you ever feel that way?"

"Ya ... of course. I guess if you let her control you, you'd be under her control."

April laughed.

"Why? What's so funny?"

"Nothing. Tell me, why did I obey her? As if her words were absolute truth," she sighed. "The burden ... do you feel them? The ache in your chest ... like you cannot *not* listen to her? You want to make her happy, but you end up sacrificing your own happiness."

"No," Jesse said. "You shouldn't feel that way."

"I thought so ..."

"What?"

They were quiet for a while until April spoke again. "I did it, you know, the divorce. I disobeyed her, and she said I had brought shame to the family—"

"No lah ..." Jesse interrupted, and as an afterthought, added, "I'm sorry."

"For what?"

"For everything that you've been through. It's not fair, you know— the divorce and then Baby Shy—"

"Baby Shy," she smiled, her eyes watery. "You remember her name."

"Of course. I didn't mean to remind you—"

"It's okay," she said, wiping her wet cheeks, and then laughed. "Remember when you got drunk for the first time? How old were you? Nineteen?"

Jesse chuckled, "I think I was eighteen. I remember it was Christmas Eve and Si Topo offered me a shot of Jack Daniel's, and after that I couldn't remember what else I drank."

"And do you remember Mama's face when she saw you drunk?" She laughed. "The second she opened her mouth to scold you, you walked past her flashing a peace sign."

Jesse laughed. "Really? No lah! I don't remember that."

"Ya! I was there, and I saw everything! Good times."

When their laughs faded, they went quiet for a long time.

"I can't believe we're finally climbing this mountain," Jesse said suddenly, looking at the mountain's silhouette as a thick curtain of mist slowly covered it.

April smiled. "Ya, we grew up under his watch, and now we get to climb him. Do you think ..." She stopped. "Never mind."

"What?"

"We should get some sleep. We start early tomorr—"

"Eh! What were you going to ask? Do I think what?"

"Nothing. It's not important."

"What the ... just say it lah!"

April paused, thinking. "Do you remember what Ninah told you about the mountain?"

"Ya, why?"

"Do you really?"

"Ya lah bah—the path of the ghosts, right?"

"Ya, a resting place before heaven," she paused. "Do you miss Ninah?"

"She's in my mind every time I'm alone with the mountain."

"Do you think we're going to see her there?"

"*See* her? I don't know. I don't think we can see spirits."

"I hope we can," April said, and then shouldered Jesse. "Seeing is not believing, and believing opens your eyes to seeing things you cannot see before. Have you forgotten that?"

Jesse chuckled, "Of course not. Are you gonna give credit to that?"

"Said by Soriling," she laughed.

"Silou totud!" Jesse said."You can't say an elder's name!"

"What are you a toddler?" April laughed.

"It's disrespectful, and she's our grandmother!"

April said nothing, smiling as she spaced out.

"What are you thinking?" Jesse asked after a while.

"Baby Shy," she said. "I need to say goodbye to her one last time at the peak."

"We're close!" April scoffed. "You go ahead lah!" She sat down on a flat rock. Flashlights of other climbers glimmered ahead of them, as though fireflies hovering along the trail.

"I would," Jesse said with umbrage. "But I don't have a flashlight." He sat down next to April. "Water?" Jesse offered after taking a quick sip. April took the bottle and guzzled a quarter of it. "Bah, let's go."

"Wait, one minute. But if you wanna go, you can go first."

"No!" Jesse stood up. "You see if we're riding a motorbike right now, I'm the one sitting at the back. I'm not in control because you're the one with the light. I can't move if you don't move—"

"What sort of analogy is that?" April laughed.

"It's a good analogy what?"

"Take this headlamp then."

"Okay, times up. Let's go!" Jesse said, pulling April up.

"But ... what about during the day?" April suddenly asked. "You don't need my light. You can see what you want and go wherever you want to go. You don't have to stick with me. You've got your own life to live."

"What nonsense are you talking about?" Jesse asked.

194

April smiled, saying nothing, and they continued climbing.

Going up the timber stairs without seeing the end of it felt like they were running an endless marathon. They stopped three times before finally reaching the end. Every time they past by someone who was resting, a sense of pride lifted Jesse's spirit.

"Don't let them catch us later," he told April. The end of the stairs was not the peak of course; it was merely a starting point to climb bigger rocks and steeper slopes. "Now, this is climbing," Jesse turned to April. "Ready?"

"Wait, my stomach hurts." April whined.

"What stomach ache!"

"Five minutes, five minutes," she urged and then sat down. Jesse had no choice but to sit down with her. They ate peanuts and raisins quietly, watching other climbers lining up, waiting for their turn to use a rope to climb a mound of giant rocks. After a few minutes of rest, Jesse felt a burn in his thighs and calves—they were too tired, too sore, and were getting soft like noodles. He thought about his bed and asked himself: *What am I doing here?* When the queue got longer, Jesse forced himself to stand up, ignoring the pain in his bones and the sourness of his muscles."Let's go!"

"Look at that," April pointed while still sitting down and chewing.

"What!" Jesse snapped.

"The moon," April smiled. "So nice ..."

Jesse looked up. A crescent moon was smiling at them, gleaming its pale, silvery ray against the ocean of black sky that was spotted with countless stars. A big silver cloud moved slowly toward the moon, as if it was Pac-Man eating a silver cherry. The Milky Way appeared like a dust-stroke across the sky, a crack where stars burst out of it. Something up there in the night sky softened Jesse's heart, calmed his spirit and overwhelmed his chest with a deep gratitude—how small he felt in that moment, how uncertain everything is.

"Do not stop here, for your way lies to the left," the mourners cried, as though chanting. The tiny white coffin at the center of the living room was adorned with white roses, and a candle stood at its foot. Before the candle burned out, another would be lit. This would continue even after the burial for seven days, symbolizing Baby Shy's spirit, lingering about the house before she left for the pinnacle of Mount Kinabalu.

"Ninah, what does it mean?" Jesse asked his grandmother, Soriling, in Dusun. They were sitting on the cold marble floor, Soriling between April and him. The villagers and mourners had occupied the rattan sofas, as well as the front yard. "What is the way that lies to the left?"

"It's the path of the ghosts," Soriling said. "They're telling Baby Shy the way to the mountain." Her wrinkly hand squeezed April's hand, but her eyes gazed inwardly into a memory. April's countenance was straight, her pasty skin was enough to inform anyone how broken her heart was. Her voice crying, *her hair is so thick like mine* lingered in Jesse's mind. They were April's words after the surgery.

"Never heard of it before," said Jesse.

"Because nobody talks about it anymore," Soriling smiled. "A lot of things have changed, but a few things like this ritual remain although it is not the same as last time. I was seven, I think, or eight when my grandfather told me about the path of the ghosts." She was quiet for a few seconds, thinking. "I've never told anyone about this before—not even your mother."

"About the path of the ghosts?"

"No... everyone knows about that." Soriling turned to Jesse. "Well, at least the folks of my generation, but not so many people know about my mother and my younger sister."

"You have a sister?"

"I *had* a sister, but like Baby Shy, she was only alive for a few minutes ... too shy to open her mouth and cry." Jesse's stomach lurched. He turned to April, who remained quiet. *Why is she not reacting to any of this?* He thought. He kept quiet, but his mind was raging—thinking carefully of what to say that wouldn't sound offensive. Soriling focused on the coffin, but she seemed to be somewhere else—perhaps visiting another memory. An urge gnawed Jesse's chest to say something to lighten up the air, but nothing came into his mind. The silence remained until Soriling said, "my mother died from giving birth to my sister. I saw her turn blue."

"Siou ..." Jesse said, "Sorry ..."

Soriling smiled, and then turned to April. "We'll get through this, April. It's not easy, but it'll get better," she said. April said nothing.

"How did you do it?" Jesse asked Soriling. "Where did you find the strength to carry on living after everything you've been through?" His heartbeat was fast, causing his voice to tremble.

"The river," Soriling said. "I went to the river to cry many times after the funeral. I thought it was a good hiding place to cry. I didn't want anybody to see me cry, but Grandfather found me one afternoon. He didn't say anything at first; he just sat next to me. We watched the river for a long time saying nothing as my tears slowly dried out." She smiled. "I still

197

remember the sound of water rushing down the stream ... the river has a healing power, but you have to decipher its language first, only then you can hear and understand their songs."

"Interesting ..." Jesse said, though he understood nothing. "Did your grandfather say anything to you after that?"

"He did. He asked me, 'Do you know where your mother and your sister are right now?' Then he pointed to the mountain. He told me after the seventh day, after the candle was blown, the spirits of my mother and my sister left to the resting place at the summit of Mount Kinabalu. He told me to stop crying because it would make them unhappy and that my tears could make them lost in the forest. If they get lost, they would never reach the summit—the resting place before heaven."

"The mountain?" April suddenly spoke. There was a spark in her eyes. "Do they really rest on the mountain's peak?"

"Yes," Soriling nodded, smiling. "Some people don't believe it, but I do. It gives me something to hold on to—a reason to move onward in life."

"What do you believe in?" Jesse asked, expecting Soriling to say Jesus or at least God because he knew his grandmother was a devout Christian.

"Everything ... everything that's true to myself."

"I don't understand," Jesse said, and thought: *But Jesus said, I am the way, the truth and the life. No one comes to the Father except through me.* "How could you believe in everything ... not only ... God?"

"Do you believe in the sun?" Soriling asked.

"Ya? You can see it ... it's out there."

"And that's your reason—because you can see it?"

"Why?"

198

"Nothing. When I asked my grandfather how the ghosts reach the mountain's summit, he said, 'by walking through the path of the ghosts.' I didn't believe it at first, but it bothered me. This was before missionaries came to introduce Jesus, which I believe in, but it didn't cancel out everything that I previously believed in ... like the path of the ghosts. It was not easy, of course, to come to this ... I mean to believe in anything at all. But when I allowed myself to believe ... like believing in what my grandfather told me, something in me transformed. I started to see things differently. It was as if something new was revealed ... like learning a new language and finally understanding a secret. I think that's what happens when you open your spirit to the spirits around you, and to the world ... to everything you choose to believe as *your* truth."

"But that has nothing to do with the sun, though. Seeing is believing. Everyone knows that," said Jesse confusedly.

"Not really ... seeing is not believing. Seeing is seeing. Believing is more than just seeing ... you can believe in things you cannot see, like the heat of the sun—you can't see it, but you believe it."

"Because you can feel heat."

"Of course, but you can't see heat, can you?"

Jesse shrugged.

"How do you prove the realness of your feelings?"

"I don't know."

"Through believing," Soriling smiled.

Jesse nodded, "Never thought of that before ... but it's the same sensation right? The heat?"

"Sure, everyone feels heat, but in different ways."

"What do you mean?"

"Look around. We are in the same room, same funeral, same experience, but the way each of us responds to it is different." Jesse frowned as he studied everyone's faces. "When you believe someone else's truth, you will start seeing things you cannot see before, and you will understand that person better."

"I don't get it," Jesse said.

Soriling chuckled, "You will one day. Our belief changes its shape all the time—like water—but shape doesn't really matter as much as the fact that water is still water."

"Tell me more about the path of the ghosts," Jesse said.

"What do you want to know?"

"Do you know where it is?"

"Well, there's a river in Kaung named Koraput that flows straight into the sea. Somewhere in the middle of the river lies a mound of large stones. My grandfather told me that this is the only place along the path of the ghosts where one can witness the ghosts passing by."

"Have you been there? Have you seen a ghost?"

"No, you can't see them, but some people said you can hear them passing by."

"Really?"

"My grandfather told me when a ghost of an old man crosses the river, he would make a sound with his walking stick, tapping on the stones. A young bachelor would make a sound of *sundatang*. A young virgin makes a soothing sound of *suling*. And when children cross the river, they would weep, and you can hear them from a great distance. Sometimes the ghosts would leave certain traces, usually on the rocks. The men would usually leave cigarette wrappers; the women leave threads, and the children would leave bits of rags."

"And you believe all this?" Jesse smirked.

"I do," Soriling smiled wistfully.

"But it contradicts the Bible."

"Maybe it does," Soriling chuckled. "But believing this doesn't mean I don't believe in the Bible. I never liked the word 'or.' I'm more of a believer in the word 'and.' There's something bigger and mysterious about this life, Jesse. Religions are like languages that guide us toward the same source of life. *Contradictions* stop us from seeing the path. You contradict day with night, but you don't choose to believe in one and not the other; you believe both day and night." She paused upon noticing Jesse's confusion. "One day, you will understand that you're free to choose, although at the same time you can't really choose."

Soriling's cold, calloused palm squeezed Jesse's wrist. It was a touch that had a beautiful splotch in his memory. "Listen, you two," Soriling said. "Sometimes when you put up you best fight, you will still lose. Sometimes you hold on to something so hard that you're afraid to let it go ... and you don't want to let it go, but you know that letting go is your only choice. Whatever it is, you need to find that courage to accept the fact. Acceptance is like floating down the stream quietly. It is easier than to go up against the current, but you still have to maneuver ... take life experiences, and build strength from them, not weaknesses. My grandfather told me this by the river that afternoon."

"Build strength, not weaknesses," Jesse whispered, listening to his pounding heart. Darkness seemed endless in the deep valley. Further ahead, lights flickered from small villages on the hills, like a cracked mirror reflecting the stars and the moon. When Jesse grabbed the rope, he jerked as the cold, wetness soaked into his cotton gloves. His fingers were freezing as he climbed up following the lights flashed from behind him.

"Are you not scared of falling?" Jesse scolded April when he saw she was not holding the rope.

"Don't talk like that. You cannot say such things here. And this rope smells like socks."

"Forget the smell. It's dangerous."

April grabbed the rope. "Fine! Satisfied?"

Jesse said nothing. Several climbers went off trail without the rope, and it made Jesse nervous as he imagined them falling off the mountain.

It was 3:42am when they reached the checkpoint. They wrote down their names in a hardcover logbook; the mountain guide told them it was for making sure everyone who passed that checkpoint would go down after 7 AM. The summit would be windy and foggy after sunrise. He then told them about a Japanese climber who went off the cliff when he ran down the slippery peak and a woman from Germany who fell off the peak while taking a selfie outside the safe boundary.

"Sometimes climbers do stupid things," the guide said. "Disobey the rules, show off how great they are, and then ended up dying." He refused the chocolate bar that Jesse offered. "Have fun and be safe," he said when Jesse and April left the checkpoint.

The climb after the checkpoint was quiet. They alternated between twenty steps and twenty seconds rest. The mountain rose sharply starting from the checkpoint—it felt like a forty-five-degree incline or more. Every time Jesse stood straight, a sensation of falling backward, tumbling down the mountain, clutched his guts. The closer he was to the mountain's floor, the safer he felt, though the anxiety had never left.

When they headed for the summit, the sky started to lighten up. Everything was drenched in a dark blue hue, and the stars started to disappear. The trail was no longer steep but tilted to the left. The wind was fiercer than before. It was so chilly that their fingers felt numb, their lips cracked, and the tip of their noses felt burnt. They were walking faster now that the real pinnacle was visible—the end of all suffering, a resting place before heaven.

"So this is the famous Donkey Ear?" April said, taking out a one-ringgit note, comparing the Donkey Ear on the money with the real Donkey Ear. She took a photo of it with her phone. "Can we stay here?" She turned to Jesse. "I don't feel like going up that peak. We're in the peak vicinity anyway."

"Okay, let's sit somewhere for the sunrise," Jesse said.

From where they were sitting, both sides of the valley and the Donkey Ear were visible. As the sun rose, the tip of its head gleamed, gilding the line where the sky and land met. It embodied the grandeur of being between heaven and earth. The golden sunray slowly poured into the cottony clouds below, as bright spectrum bathed the tenuous streaks of clouds high above the horizon. Silence lingered in the air as the wind whistled. The spirit of the sun gave life to the dead valley. Everything the sun touched seemed to come alive with vibrant colors.

"We made it," April said, her eyes glistened, reflecting the sunrise.

"Ya," Jesse smiled, taking a deep breath.

After a few minutes of silence, April said, "They're everywhere."

"What?"

"I can feel their presence everywhere. I should've noticed this earlier." She smiled at Jesse. "Baby Shy and Ninah, they're here."

"What are you talking about?" Jesse chuckled. "There wasn't any weed in those chocolate bars we just ate, right?" April ignored him, spacing out while smiling. *Where did this sudden perk come from?* Jesse wondered, and then recalled the conversation he had with his grandmother. Perhaps that was the presence April was referring to—the ghosts. Jesse felt silly for thinking about such supernatural possibilities, but the thought lingered.

When the sun's fiery body hovered above the horizon line, sunlight bathed the trail and the dark valleys. Jesse's fear of heights was amplified, stabbing his chest with every heartbeat as they climbed down the peak. April jogged downhill, hopping from one rock to another, which terrified Jesse. She was far ahead of him. He wondered where April got her energy from. Her sluggishness had completely vanished.

Jesse focused on the hard ground. Every so often he glanced at April. His stomach clenched when he heard April scream—an image of April falling off the cliff like the Japanese who ran down the mountain emerged in his mind. He felt great relief when he saw April. She was scolding a group of naked men and women who were posing in front of the Donkey Ear.

"What's this?" A *malim* with a red bandana queried. Jesse hadn't noticed them before.

"So stupid!" The other *malim* cursed, stomping on his cigarette butt before saving it in his pocket. They marched toward the nudists. Jesse followed carefully from behind, trying his best to catch up.

There were ten of them—four women and six men. The men were putting on their clothes while the women were still topless, facing toward the valley, giggling as a bearded man with a topknot snapped a photo. April was yelling and arguing with the group.

"Fuck off, woman!" A redheaded man yelled at April.

"Go back to your countries!" April yelled when two other men laughed and spoke in Dutch.

"Chill, woman. We're done!" The bearded man said, putting his camera back into his backpack.

"How would you feel if I posed naked on your mother's grave? How would you feel if I took a nude photo in your church? You fucking ignorant! Put on your clothes, *sial*!"

"Put on your clothes!" the *malim* with the red-bandana said. "You cannot do this here. It's disrespectful. This mountain is a sacred—"

"Go to hell!" The redheaded man roared. "Stupid!" He said as he walked away with the rest of the group. One of the women lifted her middle finger at them.

"Go back to your country and don't ever come back!" April shouted.

"Go to hell, bitch!" One of the men yelled back.

"Fucking ignorant!" April screamed at the top of her lungs. Her voice echoed in the cold wind. She had unlocked something else in that scream. Tears trickled down her cheeks as she kowtowed.

"What happened?" Jesse asked as he squatted next to her, catching his breath. The two *malim* were confused at April's breakdown. They might have assumed the nudists did something to her, but April refused to answer their questions—she was bawling. April's tears reminded

Jesse of the pain he'd seen after the surgery—Baby Shy sleeping breathlessly in April's arms.

"Stupid foreigner," one of the *malim* said. "Claiming to be from civilized nations ... wild boars are more civilized than them. At least wild boars know how to respect the mountain."

"Barbaric oh!" The other *malim* added. "Who do they think they are, posing naked here like they own the place? *Kitai*!"

"Right?" Jesse agreed. April wiped her wet cheeks and stood up. The two *malim* left them, deciding to go after the nudists. April said nothing for a long time. She stood frozen, looking deeply into the horizon and mumbling. Jesse caught the words "miss" and "love" from her rambles. He kept quiet, and the silence continued as they climbed down the peak and even during breakfast at Laban Rata. But when they started hiking down the mountain, April's perky self reappeared.

"Something funny you're not telling me?" Jesse asked with a smile.

"Nothing," April returned the smile. "Do you feel that time works differently here?"

"How so?"

"I don't know ... like it's not ... constricting?"

"I don't know. Is that a good thing?"

"Of course it's a good thing," she turned to Jesse. "You know if we run down the mountain, it would be less painful and faster. What do you say?" She hopped from one rock to another. "Hurry up, Jesse!" She sneered. "What are you, an old lady?"

"What the fuck?" Jesse laughed. "You go ahead lah! I'll catch up. Eh, wait!" April turned. "Do you want me to carry your backpack?"

"No need lah. I don't need you anymore," she stopped, and then turned again. "I mean ... not that I—"

"Ya, ya ... I know," Jesse laughed.

"Thank you," she smiled. "You know you're right about one thing. I was the driver, and you've just been riding on the back of my motorbike all this time."

"That analogy is no longer working. Plus, I don't need a flashlight. The sun is up."

"I know ... but look around. You have a life, Jesse. Stop being afraid to live it out; stop riding on the back of someone else's motorbike. You came up with that analogy so don't give me that face," she laughed. "By the way, in life, whether you're riding uphill or downhill, let it be glorious," she smiled.

"Credit?"

"Beyoncé!" They laughed. "And Ninah," April added. "She told me that just now."

"Just now?" Jesse giggled.

"Ya! See you at the gate!"

"Be careful!" Jesse yelled, dumbfounded with April's strange, optimistic speech. When he lifted his legs, his knees trembled and his calves cramped. "Shit!" He said, standing stock-still, watching April getting smaller every second, going deeper into the wilderness and leaving him behind. He felt lonely in that moment.

When April was no longer in sight, Jesse lifted his chin up toward the sun and closed his eyes. A delicate heat caressed his skin as a misty breeze whooshed by. He could hear the leaves and grasses slow-dancing with the wind and the birds singing and flapping their wings. The loneliness in his chest screamed, but when he opened his eyes, the sun flashed, a presence—cold and fresh—rose within his spirit, sending shivers down his spine. He felt as though something was trying to talk to him, but there was no voice. And then he felt a touch deep in his soul, which felt like his grandmother's squeeze on his wrist. He cried, overwhelmed with deep gratitude. Nobody was there, but everything seemed different, felt different, as though everything came alive for the first time. Or perhaps it was him who came alive that day.

"I see it now, Ninah," he whispered into the wind with an open heart to believe.

Another Night
by Paige Yeoh

Gritty grimy

I climb

Out from underneath

The hairy pig

Who thinks his money can

Buy me

By the hour.

He pays

for my orifices

and maybe the occasional

rough treatment

but this

hole of an existence

ends at my ass.

Only that which

I share of

My own

Free conscience

Do I grant meaning

Do I deem real

But never for them.

On the back of his motorbike

He returns me to

Silom

Maybe even to buy

Another boy

To sample us all

Before he departs.

We do not compete

Or harbor jealousy

We offer thanks with

A pity fuck

For his cash

For our families

For our freedom.

Glossary

achi murukku - Tamil: savory, crunchy snack molded into specific shapes made from rice flour that is synonymous with the Tamil Diaspora

aiya - Chinese: an expression of shock or surprise

alamak - Malay: an expression of shock or surprise

áo dàis - a Vietnamese national costume consisting of a tight-fitting silk tunic worn over pants

appam - bowl-shaped, thin Indian pancake made from fermented rice flour and coconut milk

assam laksa - a spicy and sour noodle soup dish popular in Penang

atharasam - Tamil: deep-fried, doughnut-shaped sweet that is a specialty during festivities

ay naku - Tagalog: an expression that is used when surprised, exasperated or frustrated

baju - Malay: shirt

banh mi - Vietnamese: bread

bemo - Indonesian: a minivan modified for public transport use

char kway teow - Hokkien: stir fried rice noodles with prawn, egg and bean sprouts

DBKL - Malay acronym for Dewan Bandaraya Kuala Lumpur (Kuala Lumpur City Hall)

dongquai - *Angelica sinensis*; Chinese herb used in traditional medicine for women

enduro - a long-distance race over rough terrain

gamelan - Indonesian: gong-chime orchestra found throughout the Malay Archipelago

gumamela - Tagalog: hibiscus flower

halal - Arabic: permitted according to Islamic law

halimaw - Tagalog: monster

hopia - pastry filled with mung bean paste

hor fun - flat rice noodles served in a bowl of savory soup and topped with shredded chicken and prawns

jeepney - large jeep-based public transport vehicle in the Philippines

jilbab - Indonesian Muslim woman's headscarf

kap chai - Cantonese: "little cub", named from the popular Honda Cub motorbike

kraton - Javanese: sultan's palace

kuih - general term for bite-sized snacks or dessert foods that are often steamed

lagot kayo - Tagalog: phrase meaning "you're in trouble"

lao pha - Thai: "jungle whiskey"

longi - Burmese: long cloth worn wrapped around the waist for men

malim - Malay: mountain guide

mat rempit - Malay: group of young motorbikers who race around Malaysian city streets

maya - Sanskrit: refers to the appearance or illusion of the phenomenal world *merdeka* - Malay: independence

muafakat - Arabic: consensus through discussion

munshi - a teacher usually of Indian-Muslim descent

nasi kandar - Malay: a Malaysian rice dish of Penang origins that is accompanied by curry and a variety of side dishes

pa kao ban - Thai: long cloth worn wrapped around the waist for women

peranakan - Malay: descendants of Chinese immigrants to the Malay Archipelago who have adopted local customs

pottu - Tamil: fine red powder that is applied on a Hindu woman's forehead to indicate her marital status

putu mayam - steamed Indian string hoppers made from rice flour, water and coconut milk and topped with grated coconut and palm sugar

qigong - Chinese: breathing and physical exercises related to tai chi

rambutan - tropical fruit with soft spines

ringgit - Malaysian currency

sambal - Malay: spicy chili sauce

sapatero - a person who makes or repairs shoes

sari - cotton or silk garment worn by women draped over their body

sarong - Indonesian/Malay: long cloth worn wrapped around the waist

suling - a bamboo flute

sundatang - a bamboo banjo

thúngs - Vietnamese: large round bathtubs

tongkat ali - *Eurycoma longifolia* or Longjack; shrub found in Indonesia and Malaysia that is used as a male aphrodisiac

tuk-tuk - Thai: a three-wheeled motor vehicle used as a taxi in various countries of Southeast Asia

umami - Japanese: a savory flavor

vadai - savory deep-fried Indian snack usually made from lentils and various spices

warung - roadside food stall

yong tau fu - Chinese: Hakka dish of stuffed tofu and vegetables

Contributor Biographies

Kris Williamson (http://www.kriswilliamson.com/) is a writer, editor and publishing consultant. When not writing fiction, travel narratives or poetry, he serves as director of Literary Concept, edits the Southeast Asian-themed *Anak Sastra* literary journal, and climbs volcanoes across the Pacific Ring of Fire. Or in other words, he doesn't have time to write very often.

Romalyn Ante was born in Lipa City, Philippines and moved to the UK at 16 years old. She has recently been commended in the 'Poetry' category at Creative Future Literary Awards. Her works have appeared in different magazines in the UK, USA and South East Asia, including *Under the Radar*, *Southlight* and *Ink, Sweat, & Tears*. She blogs at http://www.ripplesoftheriver.blogspot.com/.

Originally from Melbourne, Australia, **Lindsay Boyd** is a writer, personal carer and traveler who has rubbed shoulders with marginalized people of all stripes in multiple intentional communities around the world. A globetrotting veteran of more than sixty countries, he has resided and/or worked in many of them for longer periods. Home is wherever he lays his running cap.

D.R.L. Heywood-Lonsdale lives in England and grew up on the west coast of the U.S. She studied writing and literary cultures at New York University and Pepperdine University, where she received the Douglas Award for Creative Writing. Her fiction has appeared in *Anak Sastra* and her poems have appeared in *Dash*, *The Rectangle* and other journals in the U.S. and U.K.

Ipoh-born **Paul GnanaSelvam** is the author of *Latha's Christmas & Other Stories* (2013). His poems and short stories have been published both locally and internationally in e-magazines *Dusun*, *Anak Sastra*, *CQ Lit Magazine*, *The Blue Lotus*; anthologies *Write Out Loud*, *Urban Odysseys*, *Body 2 Body*, *Lost in Putrajaya*, *KL Noir: Yellow*; literary journals, *ASIATIC*, *Lakeview Journal of Arts and Literature* and *The Earthen Lamp Journal*. He currently lectures at Universiti Tunku Abdul Rahman in Kampar, Perak, West Malaysia.

Irish poet and writer **Perry McDaid** lives in Derry under the brooding brows of Donegal hills, which he occasionally hikes in search of druidic inspiration. His diverse creative writing appears internationally in the likes of *Aurora Wolf*; *Anak Sastra*; *Runtzine*; *Subprimal*; *Amsterdam Quarterly*; *Star Tips for Writers*; *Metverse Muse*; *Bunbury* and others. He is the author of the poetry collections *Ruby Silver* and *Cardboard City Opera*.

William Tham grew up in Kuala Lumpur but is now based in Vancouver, Canada, where he is the creative nonfiction editor of the *Ricepaper* magazine. He has written several short stories that have been published in various anthologies, including *KL Noir: Blue* and *Hungry in Ipoh*.

Khor Hui Min is a Malaysian book editor working in educational publishing. She thinks of life as a continuous learning process and believes in a healthy work-life balance. In her free time, she likes to write, bake, cook, blog about writing, baking and cooking, as well as volunteer with various NGOs. Her most recent publications include poems published by *Eastlit* and *The Hourglass*, and a short story published by *Anak Sastra*. You can read more of her writing at https://projectprose.wordpress.com and https://huiminskitchen.wordpress.com.

Several years ago **Don Adams** was a Fulbright scholar in Vietnam, and he has been returning to live there every summer since because he loves the city of Saigon (Ho Chi Minh City). Nine months out of the year he is a professor of English at Florida Atlantic University in South Florida, where he teaches modern literature.

Thomas De Angelo is an American writer and poet based in New Jersey. He has been in the struggling writer ranks for more years than he cares to remember. He is the author of the novel *Between the Sword and the Wall: A Novel of World War I*.

Gillian Craig is originally from Scotland, and currently lives in Singapore with her family. She has spent the last 16 years living in various parts of Asia, including Vietnam and Thailand. She has had poems published in a range of magazines, journals and anthologies, including *New Writing Scotland*, *New Writing Dundee* and *Orbis*.

Daniel T. Emlyn-Jones has written a number of short stories with Singaporean themes published in regional journals, such as *Anak Sastra*, *Quarterly Literary Review Singapore*, *Eastlit* and collected in the anthology *Yu Sheng and Other Stories of Singapore* (2015). When not writing, Daniel works as a private tutor to school children in Oxford, UK.

Ling Tan was born and raised in Kuala Lumpur, Malaysia. At the age of 21, she left for Hawai'i and later New York before ending up at Lake Atitlan in highland Guatemala, where she has lived for the last three decades. A restaurateur by vocation, she writes, paints, sings in a choir and dances in her spare time. Her piece "Thy Word Is a Lamp Unto my Feet" was published in *Anak Sastra*, while "A Tale of Three Volcanoes" appeared in *Cultural Fusions: Passions and Creativity Converging*, compiled and edited by Aaron A. Vessup. She is currently working on her memoir.

Pauline Fernandez is an analyst and photographer from Orange County, California. She has recently decided to return to the world of writing after focusing primarily on photography. Her last nonfiction piece, "Gradual," appeared in *Anak Sastra*'s 17th issue. She has also published the nonfiction story "Bittersweet" in *Mosaic Art and Literary Journal*.

Subashini Navaratnam (https://disquietblog.wordpress.com/) lives in Selangor, Malaysia and has published poetry and prose in *Quarterly Literary Review Singapore*, *Mascara Literary Review*, *Aesthetix*, *Sein und Werden*, *minor literature[s]*, *Anak Sastra*, *Jaggery*, *Halo Literary Magazine*, *Liminality: A Magazine of Speculative Poetry*, *DATABLEED*, *Deluge*, *Rambutan Literary* and *Dead King*. Her writings on books have appeared in *The Star* (Malaysia), *Pop Matters*, *3:AM Magazine* and *Full Stop*, and she has published nonfiction in MPH's anthology, *Sini Sana* as well as fiction in *KL Noir: Yellow*. She tweets at @SubaBat.

Raymund P. Reyes teaches English in Colegio de San Juan de Letran in Manila. His poetry and short fiction have appeared in *Your Impossible Voice*, *Carbon Culture*, *Torrid Literature Journal*, *Expanded Horizons*, and *Anak Sastra*, as well as in various literary journals and anthologies in his native Philippines.

Reed Venrick divides his year between Florida and Northern Thailand and usually writes poems with nature themes.

Chang Shih Yen is a writer from East Malaysia. She graduated with first class honors in English and linguistics, and with a master's degree in linguistics from the University of Otago in New Zealand. She writes a blog about footwear at https://shihyenshoes.wordpress.com/.

David Andre Davison is an American expat living in the Philippines. Some of his poems and children's stories have been published in various periodicals throughout the region. Currently, he is working on his first novel, a story based on current political tensions in SE Asia. His wife, Amy, is a professional chef and expands his waistline with delectable desserts.

John McMahon is a writer, motorcycle tour operator and sometimes antiques exporter who lives on the banks of the River Kwai in Kanchanaburi, Thailand. His writing, both fiction and non-fiction, has appeared online and in print all over the world.

Barry Rosenberg was brought up in England but moved to Australia after completing a PhD. After a few years, he became a 70s dropout, concentrating on tai chi and meditation. He started writing poetry around 1974 then moved into writing stories and plays. He currently lives on the Sunshine Coast in Queensland, where he combines writing with woodworking. From around 2008, he became active in sending material out. Since then, he has had over 25 short stories published.

Charlie Baylis was born in Nottingham. His critical writing has been published in *Stride*, *Neon* and *Sabotage Reviews*. His poetry has been nominated for two Pushcart Prizes, the Forward Prize and the Queen's Ferry Press's Best Small Fictions. He was (very briefly) a flash fiction editor for *Litro*. He has published two pamphlets: *Elizabeth* (Agave Press) and *Hilda Doolittle's Carl Jung T-shirt* (Erbacce). He spends his spare time completely adrift of reality.

A native of Rolla, Missouri, **Michael Lund** is the author of numerous scholarly publications on the Victorian novel, two collections of short stories and a number of novels inspired by *The Mother Road*, including *Route 66 to Vietnam: A Draftee's Story* (2004), *Growing up on Route 66* (1999), and *Route 66 Looking-Glass* (2014). At Longwood University in Virginia he conducts writing workshops for Home and Abroad, a free writing instruction program for veterans, active-duty military and families.

Scott Michael Reel studied English and philosophy at the University of Illinois Chicago, while also having served as a combat correspondent in the United States Marine Corps. He is currently pursuing his Ph.D. in literature and lives in Chicago, Illinois.

Tilon Sagulu is a Malaysian Dusun writer. He was born Herlveron bin Sagulu, but goes by the nickname he grew up with, Tilon (derived from a Dusun word, Guntialon, meaning "mischievous"). His works have appeared in *Laurus*, *Anak Sastra*, *Hungry in Ipoh*, *The Little Basket: New Malaysian Writing 2016*, *PJ Confidential*, *Trash*, and won the 2013 Marjorie Stover Short Story Award. He is currently pursuing a M.A in English Literature at University Malaya.

Paige Yeoh has worked in the hospitality industry for most of her life but has yet to become jaded by it. She credits infrequent opportunities to travel and even less frequent bursts of creative writing as a means to stay balanced in life ... mentally and physically. Her writing as appeared in various online journals.

See also Anak Sastra interview for this anthology at http://www.anaksastra.com/.

www.ingramcontent.com/pod-product-compliance
Lightning Source LLC
Chambersburg PA
CBHW060142130626
46556CB00006B/2459